AVENGING JESSIE

BLACK SWAN DIVISION THRILLER SERIES
BOOK 3

MISTY EVANS
NOLAN EVANS

Beach Path Publishing

ONE

Jessie

CODE SCROLLED ACROSS THE MONITOR, fast and furious. The glow lit Jessica Mendoza's face, casting sharp shadows across the angular planes reshaped by surgeons and survival. She kept her head turned slightly so the light only touched one side. The other half stayed in the dark, like the part of her soul still clawing its way back from what Harris Brewer had done.

Two in the morning inside the counterterrorism division was a symphony of silence—just the hum of servers and the occasional echo of footsteps from a security patrol. She liked it this way. No eyes on her. No pity. No suspicious whispers when they thought she couldn't hear.

Pulse keeping pace with the scrolling code, her fingers flew across the keyboard, chasing anomalies. Something had been off all night, hence why she'd stayed past her shift. There had been too many queries pinging from too many places that didn't belong. An intrusion into a restricted DOD subnet. Cloaked. Sophisticated.

And familiar.

Brewer. She leaned closer to the string of data that her program was working on. "Son of a bitch," she whispered, making certain connections that the computer software couldn't.

Her heartbeat quickened as the signature buried in the breach decrypted itself on her screen—a digital fingerprint she hadn't seen since right before Brewer had escaped custody. During her time as his minion, she'd memorized the code he used, and there it was, bold as hell.

Like he wanted her to see it.

Probably did. *Bastard.*

Accepting the challenge and his taunt, she shoved back from her desk and grabbed her tablet. The artificial lighting overhead flickered on as she passed beneath the sensors, her boots echoing across the polished floor toward Director Flynn's office.

She didn't care that it was still technically night. Flynn showed up early. Always did when something important broke. And the DOD breach was pretty damn important.

She stood outside his door, arms folded over her sweatshirt. As expected, the legend himself walked in moments later, travel mug in one hand, file folder in the other. Dark hair, matching eyes that assessed her as paused when he saw her, and an air that smacked of pure ego. "You look like hell, Mendoza."

He'd earned the right to be full of himself. As the CIA's former number one spy, he'd done things that made even her, with all of her underhanded past, cringe. "Always so full of compliments, Director. You always know how to make a girl feel good." She hugged her tablet, her hands tight on the device. "I need a favor."

He set the coffee down. "This about the breach?"

She passed him the tablet. "It's Brewer. He's back."

He yawned and rubbed his eyes. "That's why I'm here before the butt crack of dawn. Washington is on high alert. Everybody. The Pentagon, White House, the Bureau, even the Justice Department."

"This signature?" She tapped the screen. "It matches the algorithm from the Berlin servers."

"Funny thing about signatures...anyone can fake one. Or plant one." He plopped into his black leather ergonomic chair and met her eyes. "Makes me wonder why Brewer's prints keep showing up on your watch."

The accusation clawed under her skin, same as always. *Bastard number two.* Her jaw tightened, her words filled with classic annoyance. "I didn't fake this, Flynn. It's Brewer. And if you let me back in the field, I can prove it."

He didn't answer. Not directly, at least. He woke his computer and entered his encrypted passcode. "He's flexing his muscle to send us running around like chickens. It's working—he's got every ABC institution freaking the hell out right now."

"This isn't about scaring us. He's looking for something."

"Aren't we all?" He scanned his screen, his face hard as granite. "He wants to rule the world, and he's letting us know he's back on the chess board."

Adrenaline coursed through her system, making her antsy. Under his designer suit, Flynn was still an elite spy. One who understood her drive and ambition, but who'd been holding her back for the past six months since Brewer had escaped from the hospital. "He's looking for something specific. In the Pentagon."

He glanced at the signature code she still pointed to, faint purple shadows under his eyes. Like her, he wasn't sleeping, either. "Like what?"

"Could be a dozen different things. In Berlin, it was high-level security documents. But this feels different."

"We don't run on feelings, Jes."

Gold medal bastard. She regrouped, finding the words he would listen to. "I believe he's looking for the AIs." At her boss's raised brow, she continued. "Specific AIs the Pentagon uses for drones."

"So he can take control of them?"

Now, he was catching on. "Can you imagine the fallout?"

"What makes you believe he can get his hands on them?"

Feelings and hunches only, dammit. But she knew— *knew*—how Harris Brewer worked. The way his mind sorted and sifted through options and scenarios to find the one that would serve his needs. "This was a test to see if he could get in and get out without us catching him. A challenge."

Flynn *hmmed*. "A test that he failed. We know it was him, and he didn't take control of them."

She shook her head. "He couldn't get past the internal firewall."

Flynn sat back, always the devil's advocate. It sucked, but in his eyes, she saw the same old suspicion. Of her competence. Her loyalty. She couldn't blame him after the way she'd betrayed the CIA, the swans, but damn if it didn't rip up her insides every time he looked at her like that. "You're sure?"

"As sure as I am that he's a narcissistic bastard who leaves just enough of a trail so we know he's still *on the chess board*, as you called it."

He exhaled slowly. "I'll put the team on it."

She straightened. Swallowed. This was it—her break. "Not the team. Just me."

Flynn's gaze shifted from the tablet to her face again. "You haven't been cleared for field work."

"So clear me. This is *my* op, and we both know it."

He didn't even blink. "You're not ready."

"Who says?" she shot back, then forced herself to soften it. "I *am* ready. Sir."

His smile was thin, merciless. "Nice try. But calling me sir won't buy you absolution. You can call me 'sir' until the sun sets in the east, but I'm not clearing you. The Counterterrorism Center needs you."

The door opened, and Spencer Stirling walked in. Jessie straightened even more. His hair was tousled, glasses in place, and light scruff marked his jawline. His favorite laptop was tucked under one arm. It was covered in stickers, from games he played to his favorite brand of shoes.

When he looked at her, her pulse kicked. Hard.

Dammit. She turned slightly, dipping her head so her hair fell over the scars on her left side.

"Didn't expect to see you here, J." His dark amber eyes swung from her to Flynn.

She couldn't help it—her head snapped up. Why the hell not? "This is my job, too, you know."

His dark gaze roamed over her from head to toe. "Your shift ended two hours ago, didn't it?"

Flynn sat forward again, scanning his emails as he cut off her retort. "Jessie found a trace signature during the Pentagon breach overnight. Looks like Brewer."

"Already on it." Spence slid the laptop onto the desk and pulled up a window. "I intercepted a VOIP packet rerouted through an Estonian proxy just after the Pentagon reached out to Homeland. Encrypted, but the metadata led to a burner bouncing off a Munich cell tower."

Munich? "I can be ready to go in thirty minutes."

Flynn ignored her. "Can you pin down his location from it?"

Spence shook his head. "I can tell you what he's doing—what sites he's accessing, what logins he's using—but not where he is."

Jessie crossed her arms. "Great. We're drowning in data, but none of it puts eyes on him. This isn't a keyboard problem, sir," she pointedly said to Flynn. "It's a boots-on-the-ground problem. That's why you need me over there pronto."

Spence casually eyed her from over his laptop screen. "It is a keyboard problem until we track him to a physical location. That's what gets the boots on the ground. That's how we win. You remember winning, right, luv?"

God, she hated it when he called her that, his British accent getting under her skin. His cocky confidence doing the same. "Brewer knows how to vanish. You think your keystrokes are gonna catch him? We need someone who knows his tells. His psychology." Another fortifying breath. "That's me."

"Newsflash, you're not the only one who's ever gotten close enough to read him, but with you..."

His voice trailed off. His gaze snapped back to his screen.

"With me, what?" she demanded.

He sighed, raised his eyes to her. "We all paid the price."

Fury rose hot and fast inside her. She jammed a thumb at her chest. "I was the one he tried to break. The one he used her own brother against." The memory of Brewer threatening Tommy still made her guts churn. "He set me against all of you. He failed, but that makes everything he does personal to me."

Spence's jaw flexed. He didn't like being reminded of what it had cost her. Each time his gaze landed on one of her scars, it bounced away. "So, you're the avenging angel now? Brewer doesn't give a damn if it's personal to you or any of us. He only cares if he wins—and if he takes you down with him."

Bastard number three. She was racking them up this morning. "You think I don't know that?"

"Then stop acting like this is some solo redemption mission. We're a team. I know it's been a while, but you need to remember how this works. It's the Black Swan Division, not the Jessie Mendoza Vendetta Team."

She opened her mouth to fire back, but Flynn slammed his travel mug on the desk. "Enough. Both of you."

They fell silent.

Flynn finished reading another email, then rubbed his temple. "Just what I need." He pecked at his keyboard. "The interagency review committee meeting has been moved up, thanks to the breach. Kill me now." He finished his response and hit send. "Meg and Declan are heading to D.C. to check on federal infrastructure security. You two are going to Munich. Together."

What? Elation at getting her way to return to the field was quickly replaced with fury. Then the enormity of what he said hit. *Together.*

The word clanged around in her head. Her eyes flicked to Spence, who had the gall to smile. Smile! *Asshole.* "I can't work with..." She stopped herself. Felt more than saw the way Spence narrowed his eyes at her. "I can't work with *the team*. They don't trust me."

Spence snorted. He tapped the edge of a silver coin on the desk and twirled it around. A habit of his that she desperately wanted to ask him about, but never did. That would imply she cared. "That's the least of your issues. Working with me—that's your real problem."

"No arguments." Flynn sucked on his coffee, typed another fast reply, and hit send. "I need the best on this, and like it or not, you each excel at different variables when it comes to Brewer. I want you working together every step of the way. Spence is lead."

Her stomach fell to her knees. "But... That's not fair."

Flynn glared at her, and she wanted to take it back. She didn't sound like the highly trained operative he needed—that she'd been trying to convince him she was. She sounded like a three-year-old having a tantrum.

His phone buzzed with an incoming call. "It is if you want to be on the op. Take it or leave it, Mendoza. If you want back in the field, you do it my way."

Spence didn't say a word. Just closed his laptop. Pocketed that damn coin.

Jessie scowled at Flynn, then at him. The war inside her churned. Good thing she hadn't eaten anything since midnight. The abject terror she felt at working with another BSD member might have brought it up. Not just any division member—*Spencer*.

Not to mention the fact that she was about to come face-to-face with the man who'd nearly ruined her—heart, body, and soul.

Harris Brewer.

She didn't have names or curses strong enough for him.

But getting back in the field was her *dream*. Her purpose. The only thing that kept her from skydiving into madness while sitting in her boring-ass cubicle in coun-terterrorism.

This mission mattered more than her feelings. Brewer was moving again. Targeting again. She had to stop him once and for all.

For the world. For her teammates. For her friend and mentor, Tessa Vulpe, Brewer's stepdaughter, who'd lived through so much abuse from the man.

Maybe even more than Jessie herself.

If Brewer thought he could outsmart her this time...

She was about to become his worst nightmare.

And this nightmare is going to hunt you down.

"Yes, sir," she said, trying to keep the edge out of it. It didn't work. Unable to help herself, she snuck one last glance at Spence before opening the door.

Brewer was the enemy. But Spence? He was the complication she couldn't afford.

TWO

Spence

SPENCER STIRLING STARED at the screen, trying to forget the look on Jessie's face when Flynn had forced her to work with him as a condition to returning to the field.

She was brilliant, ruthless—and a liability. No one wanted her back in the field. No one wanted to work with her.

She'd been branded a traitor. Nothing official—the charges were dropped once Brewer's blackmail came to light—but the stain lingered. The fact that she could be forced to aid a terrorist was enough to make her untouchable. Most of Langley wouldn't work with her. No one wanted her on their op. Hell, most wouldn't even look at her. It had taken every Swan and Flynn himself going to bat for her just to get her clearance reinstated and land her a desk back in the building.

He hated himself for doubting her before the truth had come out. But the moment he learned she'd done it to protect her brother Tommy? That was when the bottom dropped out. He knew exactly what that felt like to choose blood over everything else, no matter the cost. She hadn't just survived Brewer. She'd sacrificed herself for family.

And God help him, that only made him fall even harder for her.

Lines of code streamed down like rain—encrypted chatter, corrupted logs, a digital breadcrumb trail buried under layers of false IPs and firewalls. In the mirrored glass of Langley's walls, he caught his own reflection—tired, wired, and already regretting not stopping Jessie before she stormed off.

Jessie...beautiful, dangerous, unpredictable Jessie. A storm front he'd learned not to stand in the way of.

Flynn had done the right thing. Working alone might have sent her into a spiral. A dark hole of revenge that she might never come out of.

He'd had more intel to share with her and Flynn before she stormed out of the director's office. He'd shared it with Flynn, who'd then been summoned by Deputy Director Michael Stone into a meeting. The situation was escalating fast.

Flynn's assistant was working on their flights. Spence was waiting for her to give the go-ahead that they were ready.

With a tight exhale, he pushed away from his desk and headed down the corridor, weaving past early-shift analysts and operatives. Jessie's cubicle was a closet-sized corner of the counterintelligence floor, wedged between a storage room and the stairwell. She liked it that way— isolated, out of the flow, forgettable. Even after six months, she wasn't ready to be seen again.

But he *saw* her. In ways she hated.

He paused, peering over the blue freestanding partition panel, his height making it easy for him to see over the top. The flickering overhead light gave her a spectral edge. She was already packing gear, stuffing her laptop and zip ties, along with a handheld scanner, into a weathered bag. Her back was rigid, her movements precise. Another of her coping mechanisms, he'd learned. The armor she always wore.

"You're wasting your time," she said, not looking up. She had an uncanny sense when he was near. "I don't need backup. Why don't you stay here with Meg and Declan? They need you more than I do. Be useful where you're comfortable, Spence."

A jab and twist of the knife. "Yeah, well, I'm not backup." He filled the threshold, crossing his arms. He was damn tired of having to justify his presence on the team with her. "I'm mission-critical."

Jessie zipped her duffel with unnecessary force and snorted. "We need to confront Brewer face-to-face, which means physical access to him. You can't gain that playing Minesweeper from a van."

Spence's jaw ticked. He stepped fully into the cubicle, tamping down his irritation. "You think that breach at the Pentagon happened because someone guessed the admin password? I've been tracking that signature for weeks, all over Europe and our embassies. The AIs he's after have ties to ones I designed three years ago and never should have left the lab."

She finally looked at him. Her gaze wasn't dismissive. It was defensive. Like she'd been backed into a corner and didn't want him to see the bruises.

Or her scars.

He hated that look.

"Let me guess," she said, grabbing a pen light that was much more than a pen light. "You want to come along to prove you're not just a desk guy."

Was she deliberately pushing him away, or was she simply testing him? "You know I'm not just a desk guy. I've been in the field more than you have. I'm going because I built the thing Harris is after." Spence stepped closer, voice low. "If he gets access to that AI, we're not talking EMP attacks. We're talking autonomous sabotage. The kind of system that can learn how to tear apart infrastructure in real-time. Power grids. Stock markets. Defense satellites. It could literally take down our government in the blink of an eye."

Jessie flinched and hesitated, her fingers stalling over a flash drive.

Spence pressed on. "The Pentagon breach is a test. He's probing vulnerabilities—figuring out how far he can go without setting off every alarm from here to NORAD.

The moment he integrates it, we're blind and bleeding before we know we're hit."

Jessie's brow furrowed. "Don't be dramatic. Your AI was decommissioned."

"That's what they told me, but I know that design."

She caught his drift. "Your ego is so big, you think your version is the only one he would go after."

Low blow, but more defensive than cruel. A retort was on the end of his tongue, but he held back. He needed her to trust him. To want him as her partner on this mission. "It *was* decommissioned, and I was told the software was destroyed." A memory of the last time he'd seen the code in action and the failed mission that had resulted from it made him cringe inwardly. Man, he'd created a lot of shit in his time, most of it he considered failures. "This isn't about my ego. I know that code. Harris has a copy—and he's feeding it government-grade security data."

She straightened, the weight of her duffel tugging at her shoulder, as she went all agent-mode. "You should've told Flynn."

He tried to catch her eye to make sure she understood the stakes. "I did. And the fallout is already starting. That's the real reason why Flynn is sending us together, J."

Her lips parted, but she didn't speak. His eyes rested on her near-perfect lips. The rest of her face was unreadable, but those lips... Yeah, he could read them like his own thoughts. "No one in their right mind wants to work with me."

Ah, and there it was—the crux of the matter. "I do."

Her eyes met his. Skirted away. "You're a fool."

His phone buzzed before he could argue. It was a text from Flynn's assistant. Jessie's phone buzzed right after his, probably with the same message. The flights were booked.

"Clock starts now," Jessie muttered, tapping her smart watch to start a timer.

"Look," he said. "I get it. You want to do this mission solo because you think this is your chance to make it right. I get that, but you don't have to do this alone. We're a team. Again. Like we were when Black Swan first started."

She looked away. Not out of weakness, but because she never held his gaze for long. He wasn't sure if it was because she knew he had a crush on her or because facing him was too raw. Too real. She couldn't face her failures, and he reminded her of them.

And God, he hated being that reminder. What woman in her right mind would want him around if he caused her to remember the worst time of her life every damn time she looked at him?

"I work better alone," she said.

"Maybe." He shrugged. "But I don't."

Her chin snapped up. A strained silence stretched between them. He met her glare and the silence head-on. It continued to expand, taut, sharp, and threaded with the things they never said.

Finally, she brushed past him into the hallway. "I'll meet you at the airport."

Spence turned to follow. "We could—"

"No, we can't, Stirling."

With clenched fists and squared shoulders, she left him standing there. The sound of her boots faded down the corridor.

He stayed where he was, watching her go. He could hack firewalls and trace digital ghosts across five continents. But Jessie Mendoza? She was the one code he'd never cracked.

"But I will," he promised himself. Spencer Stirling was no quitter. Not when he wanted something. And he wanted her. "I most certainly will."

THREE

Jessie

THE SKY over Munich was a sullen bruise, thick with the promise of rain. Gray clouds hung low, diffusing the late afternoon light and casting the city in cold hues of concrete and steel. Jessie adjusted her scarf higher around her neck and scanned the park's perimeter. She didn't like meeting in open places. Too many angles. Too many ways to get dead.

Spence sat on the bench beside her, legs crossed, phone in hand, playing his part perfectly. To anyone watching, they were just another couple killing time on a stroll.

But Jessie's pulse thrummed with that familiar edge of readiness, her gaze ticking between the dog walkers, the joggers, the man with the newspaper who hadn't turned a page in five minutes.

A woman in a trench coat approached, her stride purposeful but casual. She dropped onto the opposite end of the bench without a word and set down a paper bag.

"It's the only thing I could get." Her voice was soft as she typed on her phone as if responding to a text. "Topographic layout of the compound outside Görlitz. Just remember, you didn't get it from me."

Jessie sat between them, digging in her backpack as she muttered, "We never met."

The woman tucked her phone in a coat pocket. "Brewer's got an ally in town. Jonas Keller. "

"Who the hell is that?" Jessie asked, frowning into her open bag.

The woman checked her watch. "Low-profile financier. Tied into gray-market contracts all over Europe. Berlin thinks he's bankrolling Brewer's projects. He'll be at the Bundestag Initiative gala tomorrow night. His name's on the donor list."

Spence glanced up from his phone and yawned. Jet lag had them both in its claws. "Gala, huh? Will Brewer be there?"

The woman snorted and rose, making a show of tightening her trench coat belt. "He doesn't show his face in public." It was said with a *duh* tone in her voice. "Otherwise, we'd already have caught him."

She vanished into the foot traffic. Jessie casually snatched up the paper bag and stuffed it into her backpack.

Back at the hotel, the air inside their connecting

suites smelled like stale carpet and industrial cleaner, and the heat was too high, drying out her throat and temper. Jessie stripped off her jacket and tossed it onto the bed. She hadn't unpacked. She didn't plan to be here long.

Spence, leaning in the doorway that connected their rooms, had his laptop balanced on one forearm and his phone in his other hand. He watched her like a man studying the edges of a minefield. Yet, he still seemed unbothered. Totally confident. It made her want to throw something.

"I did a little digging." He strolled across the carpet and dumped his gear on the white French provincial-style desk. "That gala is at the Bayerische Staatsbiblio-thek—State Library, right in the heart of the city. Black-tie. Security's tight, but not impossible to breach. Especially if we have an invitation."

Jessie shook her head and dug the paper bag out of her backpack. Inside was a manila envelope. "Unless you've got a tux stashed in your fancy suitcase, I don't see that happening."

He grinned without looking up, his fingers flying over his keyboard. "Even better. We go as a couple. Pretend we're donors. Maybe even get a dance or two in while we track Keller."

She was about to grab the map from the envelope, but stopped. "Are you serious?"

"Deadly."

"That's your big plan? Posing as a power couple at a gala?"

He finally looked up. "It's the easiest play. We blend in. Get close to Keller without raising red flags."

She opened her mouth to argue—but he turned the laptop toward her. A grainy photo filled the screen. "This is our guy," he said.

Keller, smiling in a gray tailored suit, was posing and shaking hands with a German telecom CEO. Her stomach fled south to her toes. "That's not Jonas Keller."

"What?" Spence double-checked the screen. "That's what it says." He read off the man's bio listed in the article.

She might not have recognized the change in his hair or the plastic surgery he'd had done, but she knew those eyes. *Hastings*.

Jonas fucking Hastings.

The room tilted, and she dropped the envelope onto the bed. Her breath stuck in her lungs. Memories of failure, of betrayal, came rushing back.

Seeing her reaction, Spence straightened. "What's wrong? Who is he?"

Jessie sat heavily on the edge of the blue and white striped comforter. "He was my first handler, Jonas Hastings. He trained me. Used me. Then vanished. Langley suspected he was leaking intel. They gave me an off-the-books op to confirm it. My first mission was investigating my own handler as a traitor."

Spence stilled. "What happened?"

So many years ago now. So much had happened. "Doesn't matter." She stiffened her spine. "I can take him down with Brewer."

Spence shifted in the chair. "It does too matter. I need the details. This mission isn't about him, and if he's going to blow the op, I need to know."

She wouldn't let him. Her fingers fiddled with the manila envelope. "I got close to him back then. He realized I was on to him, and that's when he disappeared." A derisive laugh left her lips. "I blew my first official mission, so yeah, he knows me. If he sees me at the gala, we're blown before we even get started."

Spence was quiet for a long moment, then shut the laptop. "He's reinvented himself as Jonas Keller."

She rubbed her eyes. "He's changed his appearance, but that's him. I'm sure of it. And apparently, he's working with Brewer." She let out a huff. "God, I never would've thought the two of them would team up, but the truth is, they're a lot alike."

Spence paced, rubbed his hands together. Glanced out the window. "If he's allied with Brewer, the gala's still our best shot at tagging him and figuring out where Brewer is."

"No," she said, pushing to her feet. "We'll find another way."

"Jess—"

"He'll make me. Besides, I'm not going into that place pretending to be some giggling arm-candy while the man who nearly wrecked my career before it even started sips champagne."

Spence kept his tone neutral. "He won't even see you if we do this right. You want justice? This is how we get it. You're just as skilled as anyone at changing your appearance."

"No," she snapped again. "Don't you get it? I blew my assignment with him, and now he's teamed up with my archenemy. I'm not going to blow this mission to bring down Harris Brewer by getting sidetracked by that asshole."

He stepped closer. "You're not twenty-three anymore. Not a rookie. You can handle Hastings, and I'll handle Brewer. Think of it as a two-fer." He shot her a grin. "Commodations will land in both our files, and Meg, Declan, Tommy, and Tessa will be pissed that we brought in two traitors instead of one."

While her insides turned, she locked down all expression. "I told you before, I work alone."

"You survive alone. That's different."

That hit like a blow to her chest. She turned away. Her skin felt too tight. Her thoughts raced. She hated the idea of being seen. Of wearing a dress. Of letting him see her bare skin. Her scars.

Yes, most had healed and were barely visible now, but... "We'll track Hastings once he leaves the gala at the end of the night. That way, we don't have to risk having our covers blown and alerting Brewer we're in town."

Spence watched her, and when he spoke again, it was softer. "It's not Hastings you're afraid of. It's being seen."

Even her guts froze. Why wouldn't he leave her the fuck alone? "You're not my shrink."

"Well, you need one, since you stopped going to Dr. Kumar six weeks ago. Not that he was doing you much good, but perhaps you should consider finding someone else. Someone who can help you with your body issues, as well as your emotional ones."

"How dare you?" She flung out an arm and pointed at the door. "Get out."

"Jessie, I'm sorry. That was uncalled for." He took a step toward her, then stopped when she backed up. He raised placating hands. "I know you're doing the best you can."

Oh, my God. Seriously? That was even worse. And within those words was a question in Spence's mind— why had Flynn cleared her for fieldwork?

Fuck. She had to prove to Spence that she could do this. She hadn't wanted him for a partner, but now that he was here, a lot was riding on his opinion. On what he would report back to Flynn.

She sure as shit didn't want him digging around in her head. She'd always admired how smart he was—street smart as well as tech savvy—but now, it was like nails being driven into her back.

She steeled her voice. "Everyone thinks I'm broken, but here's the truth—what happened to me has made me stronger and more resilient. I'm a better spy than any of you because of it. So, I don't need a partner, and I especially don't need one who thinks I'm just *doing my best*. Why don't you pack up your laptop and go back to Langley, where you belong?"

His eyes went hard, and he strode toward her until he was towering over her. "I'm exactly where I belong. *With you.* I'm on your side. Always. But you can't do this if you're still bleeding inside. You were never like this before, and I know the old you is still in there. Yes, you went through something extremely traumatic, but you're not the only one in this room who's had people screw you over."

She was well aware of his background on the streets of London as a young boy. About a mentor who had adopted him and two other boys and turned them into weapons. How they had been groomed to help the Mastermind, an evil man who'd been part of a shadow government, and how Spence and his adopted brothers had been forced to take down the only father any of them had ever known.

It still didn't give him the right to say these things to her. "Go to hell, Stirling."

He gathered up his hardware and didn't look at her as he walked out. The door clicked shut behind him.

She stood there alone, pulse hammering, fists clenched, eyes burning. The past wasn't done with her yet.

And neither, apparently, was Spence.

FOUR

Spence

HE WRESTLED with pulling the plug on the gala visit all night, pacing and listening to what went on beyond the other side of their connecting doors.

He expected her to sneak out. To go off on her own.

She didn't.

Which surprised the hell out of him.

The next morning, he was still debating. Not only the gala, but the op itself. He could track down Brewer on his own, but he didn't want to. Brewer was Jessie's Achilles' heel. She needed to be the one to capture the man and send him to prison if she was ever going to find closure.

Nursing bad coffee from the room's coffee pot, he nearly had a heart attack when the door banged open. She didn't knock—just barged in through the connecting door between their suites like she owned both rooms and the air in between.

Coffee spilled over the rim of the heavy white mug, burning through his shirt. He sat up too fast and blinked up from his laptop. "Jessie—?"

"We're going to the damn gala." She did a heel turn, already halfway back out. "Get ready."

The door slammed before he could ask what had changed her mind.

He stared at the space she'd just filled, her voice echoing in his skull. He'd expected more verbal sparring. Another wall. Not this about-face. Had she changed her mind because of what he'd said—or was she just angry enough to prove she wasn't afraid?

Either way, she was walking straight into danger— and he wasn't sure he could watch her do it.

He swore under his breath, launched himself out of the desk chair, and tapped into a secure server to hack the gala's guest list. The Bundestag Initiative maintained a tight list of tech donors and political figures. Posing as cybersecurity consultants from a high-level firm took finesse, but he could spoof credentials in his sleep.

He cracked the guest registry through a shell proxy, splicing in some fake credentials while pretending not to notice that his hands were shaking.

His cover alias: Spencer Worth, CTO of Sentinel Defense.

Hers: Jayla Worth, his brilliant and beautiful wife.

He paused long enough to wince at that. Jessie would hate it. Hate him.

What's new? He uploaded the forged invitation and fired off a rush order with the hotel's concierge for a tailored tuxedo to be delivered within the hour. It wouldn't be designer, but with his build, he knew how to make it look like it.

He was just finishing when a soft knock echoed from the connecting door.

When he opened it, a dangerous hallucination was standing there.

The gown was black satin, cut sharp and sleek, slit to the thigh, and sleeveless. It fit her like it had been molded to her curves. Her heels made her several inches taller, bringing her up to his own height.

Her eyes—no, not her eyes—contacts, he realized. They were a deep emerald, disguising her hazel color, and rimmed in charcoal. Her lashes were already thick, but she'd added a layer of falsies to call even more attention to them.

He hadn't seen her wear makeup since Vienna. What she'd done with concealer and blush had sculpted her features just enough to soften the angles—contour over her cheekbones, shadow to recede her jaw. But it was still her. Fierce. Battle-forged.

And drop-dead gorgeous. He tried to say something. Failed.

"I stole it off the rack of dry-cleaned clothes a maid was delivering to various rooms." She held up a dark auburn wig. "I need help with this. I can't get it to stay put. I don't want to color my hair, so a wig is the answer.

The shop downstairs had a slim selection. Above all else, I cannot let Keller recognize me."

He tried to speak again. His tongue tripped over itself.

"Spence?"

Swallowing hard and turning away so she didn't notice what was going on down below in his pants—*hello, instant erection*—he gestured for her to enter. "Yeah, yeah. Come in."

She stepped across the threshold, hesitant this time. The scent of lemon and eucalyptus followed. She didn't look around, didn't comment on his frantic effort to make the room presentable. Just walked straight to the bathroom with the wig, a hairbrush, and a handful of pins.

He followed, heart thudding like a live grenade in his chest. This was why emotional entanglements were off-mission. They scrambled the brain. *Danger assessment*: fucking off the charts.

When he joined her in the luxurious bathroom, the open space suddenly felt like close quarters. He fidgeted with his hands, not knowing what to do with them. His attention kept straying from the deep V of the dress that exposed her vulnerable spine to her tight shoulders. And then there was the delicate curve of her neck...

"Spence?" She frowned at him in the mirror. "Are you okay?"

Snap out of it, he ordered himself. He returned to the main room and grabbed a barstool from the breakfast nook. "Here," he told her, setting it next to her. "You sit. I'll fix it."

He wasn't sure how. While he'd had training in using disguises, he'd never made over a female accomplice before, and he sure as hell wasn't sure what to do with a wig.

She eased onto the stool, back straight, eyes locked on her reflection. He grabbed the brush and started smoothing down her dark hair. It was shorter than when he'd first met her, back when they'd both been younger, more at ease with their jobs, and eager to do them. Not younger in years, but in their perspectives.

All that had changed when Mosai Hagar had kidnapped her and Meg. Before Jessie had been killed on camera during a live stream to the entire world.

Except, it had been a deep fake. Not the kind where AI was used to mimic her death, but one where another woman who had an uncanny resemblance to her had been beaten to the point she wasn't recognizable and put in Jessie's place. Not that Jessie hadn't been beaten to a pulp, too, but she'd been saved from death by Harris Brewer and forced to work for him by threatening to kill Tommy.

Spencer had always known Jessie was loyal to the CIA and America. But those loyalties could be broken. The one to her brother could not. She'd endured everything Brewer had thrown at her in order to keep Tommy safe.

Not only did Jessie live with those terrible memories and the ongoing aches and pains from bones and soft tissue injuries that had never healed properly, she also wrestled with the fact that they had used an innocent woman to take her place.

It was truly no wonder that she had so many hang-ups. That she was always on a knife's edge, and in constant fight mode. He couldn't begin to imagine what went on in her head most of the time, and he was grateful that she hadn't taken a razor to her wrist or downed a bunch of pills, no longer able to handle the demons that haunted her day and night.

Her hair was soft under his fingers. While she used to keep its natural wave flattened, these days, she used the waves to hide behind. Surgical scarring at her temples peeked through the strands when he brushed too deeply.

She didn't flinch. He did.

"What's the plan for tonight?" she asked, her voice level.

He cleared his throat, using several of the pins to tame her thick locks. "Whatever circles Keller is running in, Brewer is, too. Tonight is about putting eyes on Keller to see who he interacts with, who he buddies up to. The gala is the perfect place for him to recruit backers and secure other resources to put Brewer's plan in motion. I'll handle gathering the identities of those whom Keller seems particularly interested in tonight. You're only job is to keep an eye on the security team the gala has hired and make sure no one gets suspicious of us."

"So I'm just the lookout? Babysitting you while you chase the bad guys?"

"I'm telling you not to bleed for Brewer. Not again." He

didn't say what he really meant—that watching her bleed the first time nearly gutted him. That every time he noticed her scars—which was less and less these days, but still—it gutted him all over again. "You got away from him once. There's no way in hell I'm letting you end up under his thumb again."

She stilled. He met her eyes in the mirror, and something hot twisted in his gut.

"I'm not incompetent. The last thing I'll ever do is let that happen."

He held her accusatory gaze. "Keeping an eye on security and keeping our asses out of jail, or dead in some back alley, it's just as important as gathering intel on Keller and Brewer. I need you to watch my backside. There's no one else I'd rather have doing it, either. You know Brewer. You know Keller. Which sucks and all of that, but it's a bonus for us. Do you understand that? You are the key to taking down two major traitors to the CIA. You can stop a global war that will cripple the United States. *You, Jessie.* In this partnership, on this mission, you're the most valuable asset we have. You're the key to everything."

He saw her throat bob as she swallowed. Her gaze fell to the sink. "Yes, I am, and yes, I know how important it is to make sure security doesn't get a whiff of what we're doing."

He couldn't help it, as he resumed his work, his fingers brushed the curve of her neck. She didn't move, but her gaze returned to watch him. He didn't meet her gaze directly, fooling with securing the wig with multiple bobby pins, and judging whether or not it looked real enough.

It did. It was a high-quality product, and its color brought out her eyes even more. He messed with a couple of tendrils, admiring his work. Admiring her. She rose, leaning toward the mirror to examine his handiwork as well. Her spine was totally exposed to him, the fabric of the dress molding over her ass.

He needed to take a step back.

He didn't.

She turned to face him. Too close. She was way too close, those enormous eyes and her delicious scent sucking him in. He could see the pulse fluttering in her throat.

Her lips parted, then closed like she didn't trust the words forming on her tongue. "Thank you," she said quietly.

"You look..."

She lifted a brow. "Don't."

"Right." He could hear his own pulse pounding in his ears. Could see the moment where she almost said something else. Nearly leaned into him.

A knock shattered the moment, and they both shifted.

She was instantly on alert, on edge again. "Who's that?"

Of all the terrible timing. His gaze went to the clock on the wall. "Room service. They're delivering my suit."

Jessie blinked, stepped away from him, and headed for her room. "Hurry. We don't want to be late."

He didn't stop her, but he wanted to. Wished he could ask her to stay—even if it was only to breathe the same air a minute longer.

When the adjoining door clicked shut, he could've sworn he heard her pause on the other side with a whoosh of relieved breath.

He smiled to himself. Maybe he wasn't the only one coming apart at the seams.

His hand drifted to his pocket, fingers closing around the worn edge of the coin. *Don't lose it, mucker. Don't lose her.*

FIVE

Jessie

BACK IN HER SUITE, Jessie ripped off the heels first—obscene things—and dropped them like twin daggers onto the carpet. Her feet already ached from wearing them after only a few minutes. How was she going to make it for hours at the gala?

Her shoulder blades were pinched from the tension of pretending. Pretending to be calm, charming, and beautiful. How unnatural that had felt. Once, she'd never doubted her looks and what they could do for her, in the field or in her personal life. Now she didn't see herself in the same way, and never would again.

The worst, however, had been pretending she hadn't wanted to lean into Spence and kiss the hell out of him when he finished pinning her stupid wig.

She cursed under her breath and yanked the drawer

on the nightstand open, pulling out her go-kit. Comms, listening devices, miniature trackers, a lipstick camera. She sorted them to calm her nerves and prepare for the evening ahead, each device offering a measure of control she no longer felt in her bones. She'd trained for chaos. But tonight felt personal, and that could make her sloppy.

"You let him in too far," she muttered, shoving another tracker into her satin clutch. "Should've kept your guard up. Should've shut the damn door and bolted it before you let him touch you."

But she hadn't. And now they were playing dress-up together, and somehow, it mattered. Not just for the mission. Not just because of Keller or Brewer. It mattered because when Spence looked at her the way he just had, he saw the woman underneath the bruised loyalty, the fractured pieces. He didn't flinch at the scars. He admired the fire.

A knock sounded from the connecting door.

"It's time," he said, voice steady.

Her fingers froze on the clasp of her clutch. She took a deep breath and counted to ten.

Another knock. "J?"

Pressing her lips together and steeling her spine, she went to the door, opened it, and froze.

He looked like he'd walked out of a billion-dollar gala advertisement—tailored tux hugging lean muscle, his dark hair slicked back just enough to highlight cheek-bones that should be illegal. His eyes scanned her in return, as if memorizing the woman who now wore blush instead of blood.

Her pulse was skipping far too fast, and her breath felt stuck in her chest. She cleared her throat and yanked her emotional armor into place as she tugged the shoes from hell back on. "Well, you clean up all right."

He smirked. That grin, so full of himself, made her knees weak. "You're the one who's going to turn heads. Ready to ruin some folks' nights?"

"Hell, yeah."

He extended his arm. It was a small gesture. Civilized. Gentlemanly.

And it felt like stepping off a cliff—without a parachute.

Jessie hesitated, kicking herself for feeling so...scared. Touching him, acting like his wife, it was too much.

And something she still had to do.

She yanked the armor closer. Layered more on. Then she slid her hand into the crook of his elbow.

The strength there was steady. Trustworthy. She hated how much she liked it. When was the last time she'd leaned on someone? *Too long.*

The limo waited downstairs, sleek and black. The drive to the gala passed in a blur of streetlights and nerves. Spence went over their cover stories ad nauseam, but she could barely concentrate, the feel of him next to her overwhelming. He was wearing a subtle cologne of leather and cedar that teased her senses, making it hard to focus.

The ballroom sparkled and sucked them in. Gilded chandeliers, violins humming overhead, glittering gowns, men with medals and bloodstained secrets. Women with diamonds and claws.

"Let's mingle," Spence said.

He scanned for Hastings, and she analyzed security, being the good little operative he wanted.

She spotted Hastings near the bar—older, leaner, but the smile was the same. Smug. Predatory. Hunting for the next fool to manipulate. He rubbed his ruby ring, checked his phone compulsively. *Just like he used to.*

Her skin crawled. Her stomach twisted. "He's here." She kept her back to the traitor. "Ten o'clock."

Spence casually glanced toward the bar. His body stiffened. "Shit. He's heading this way. We can't let him see you."

"I've got this—"

"Jess." He caught her jaw and leaned in. "Play the role."

And then he kissed her.

It wasn't soft. Wasn't slow. It was strategic. A distraction. A cover.

And it set her entire nervous system on fire.

She wanted to shove him. Or maybe pull him closer. Her brain scrambled. This was *wrong*—it wasn't supposed to matter. But the way his hand gripped her hip, the way his lips moved against hers...

All logic fled. She kissed him back. Just for a second. Just enough to sell the lie.

Just enough to lose control. To fall into his embrace, his mouth, and forget...

He pulled away, studying her face. Her breathing

was fast. He ran a gentle hand along her arm. "You okay? I had to make him think you were just a trophy wife."

Jessie blinked, tried to call up her best glare. Her voice seemed to have deserted her, but when it did finally show up, it came out breathy. "Next time, warn me before you shove your tongue in my mouth."

He smirked. "Are you complaining?"

His touch was reassuring, but she still felt queasy as Hastings, acting as Keller, greeted someone a few feet away. She drew back ever so slightly as unbidden memories from before Hastings' betrayal mauled her. She reached for a comeback that would mask her tumble of emotions. "I'll put it in my mission report."

Spence smirked and squeezed her elbow. "I'd believe that if your voice didn't crack. Seeing him must be a kick in the stomach. Are you sure you're okay?"

Hastings had been so charming, so sincere when he'd taken her under his wing. And even though he was a traitor, she'd learned a lot from him during their months together. He'd taught her spycraft and built her confidence in herself before everything went to shit and she learned his true character. "I will be."

Needing air, she peeled away to weave through the crowd and find a quiet place to observe. She expected Spence to pull her back, but he didn't.

Security wore all black, with obvious earpieces lending them credibility. They weren't amateurs. She needed to stay sharp and focus on them, rather than Hastings—or her bloody, inconvenient attraction to Spence.

Clocking all the security guards in sight, she didn't notice any acting suspiciously. After a few minutes, she grew bored but kept tailing the most elite of the group.

None made any motions toward her or Spence.

Two men near the corner of the ballroom caught her attention. Both were ex-military types, all square jaws and lazy confidence. She angled behind a group of drunk patrons making a commotion, slid past a couple leaving the dance floor, and positioned herself near them. She could eavesdrop on them while still watching the half dozen posted security guards in the ballroom.

They spoke low, heads tilted toward their drinks and each other. "It's almost ready," one said. "They just need the targeting software. AI handles the rest. The drones are at the compound."

The compound?

Görlitz. Their asset had come through on that front.

The second man swirled his drink and stared at a gorgeous, model-thin woman on the dance floor. "Autonomous drones?"

"Smaller than a hawk, faster than a bullet. Facial recognition at five hundred yards."

Jessie's blood iced over. She pulled out her lipstick and snapped covert photos of both men with the camera. Every spy instinct screamed for her to move, but this was her one chance to capture them. She sent the images via encrypted signal to Spence with a message. *Two guys at the bar, talking drones at a compound. Could be the lead we need.*

Spence replied almost instantly. *Meet me in the corridor by the coat check.*

She moved, leaving her cover behind, and stuck the lipstick cam in her bag. She kept her eyes forward, her posture elegant, and made sure every step was disguised in grace.

A man in a tux, bulging around his middle, asked her to dance. She politely turned him down. A waiter nearly backed into her with a tray of champagne. Someone else stopped her to ask if she knew where the ladies' room was.

Every time, she felt panic bloom right below her breastbone. It was becoming increasingly difficult not to drop her cover and flee.

Once she reached the plush, carpeted entrance hall, the noise became muffled. She pressed her back against a wall and forced herself to take deep breaths. One, two, three. *I can do this.*

She pushed off and headed for the coat check.

A hand snagged her wrist as she passed an empty hallway. "Not so fast."

It was one of the men. The taller one with the hawk tattoo on his neck. He yanked her toward him, making her trip in her heels, and shoved her inside a service room before she could scream.

"Your purse," he demanded, holding out his hand.

This was going to get ugly. He outweighed her by eighty pounds or more and towered a good six inches over her. He could probably kill her with a single blow, and still be out the door before security blinked.

She straightened, ignoring the pain in one of her ankles from twisting it. Tucking her pocketbook under her arm, she blinked her eyelashes at him and gave him her best innocent look. "Excuse me?"

He smacked her hand away from the purse and jerked it from its spot under her armpit. "Give me your goddamn purse. I saw you taking pictures. Who the hell are you?"

"Geez, take it easy. I took a picture of you because I thought you were cute." She grabbed the bag, which resulted in a tug of war with him. "Don't be an asshole."

He slapped her, snapping her head back into the wall and stunning her. Stars danced in front of her eyes. "Don't lie to me, bitch. Who are you? Who do you work for?"

Damn. So that's how this is gonna go down. Blinking, she scanned the room, searching for a weapon. That was the only way she could level the playing field.

There were plenty of potentials, but her best option was the one she had on her. "Go to hell."

She kicked his shin and went for the knife strapped to her thigh beneath the slit of her dress.

He was fast, though, anticipating her moves. He slammed her against the wall, bringing up a beefy arm and pressing it to her throat. His other hand flicked out a knife, smaller than hers but equally deadly. "Nice try."

She jammed the butt of her palm into his nose, ducked under his arm, and scrambled past him. He grabbed her by the waist. She slashed with the knife, catching his bicep, and staggered as he clipped her shoulder with his.

Pain flared, sharp and bright to match her stinging cheek and blurry vision. She stumbled but didn't fall. When he lunged again, she caught him between his legs with her knee.

He collapsed to the floor with a strangled curse, dropping the knife.

Jessie stood over him, shaking and ready to do more damage with hers, when Spence burst in. "Jess!"

"Got it handled," she said, breathless and blinking away the spots in her vision.

"Fuck." He eyed the guy, who was holding his balls and groaning, and turned to her. "What the hell happened?"

"He didn't like me taking his picture." She retrieved her purse and staggered on her bad ankle. Spence reached for her elbow, keeping her from falling. "If we let him live, he'll cause trouble."

The asshole was lurching to his feet. Spence propped her against a shelving unit, stepped forward, and kicked the brute in the head. The guy went down for the count, his eyes rolling up in his head. She didn't flinch, but something in her chest squeezed at the sound of the man's skull cracking tile.

His body spasmed once and stopped moving. Spence scanned her from head to toe. "You're hurt."

With quick, calm movements, he grabbed a clean cloth from a stack of towels on the shelf and some hand sanitizer. He cleaned the cut on her shoulder, every movement professional.

His hands brushed her skin, but there was nothing sexual in it—just care. "We're compromised. We need to get out of here pronto and go underground."

Jessie nodded, trying to force away the dizziness. His lips were close enough to kiss. The nod cost her, making the spots flare and the pain in her cheek burn. "Let's move."

Spence retrieved their coats, and she only put her shoes back on long enough to walk to the limo. Her eyelid twitched, and she fought the urge to curl into him and sleep. "I may have a concussion," she admitted through gritted teeth.

He took her chin between his fingers and thumb and forced her to meet his gaze, studying her pupils. "Anything else I should know about?"

Plenty, but she didn't have the energy to tell him. "I'll be okay. I just need a minute to regroup."

The physical violence had been bad enough, but the PTSD that surfaced thanks to what Mosai Hagar had done to her was worse.

She shivered, and Spence pulled her close, tucking her head under his chin. "I've got you. You're safe now."

If only that were true. She knew it wasn't, but she appreciated him saying it anyway.

Back at the hotel, they didn't speak. Spence made sure their rooms weren't compromised and then asked her if she was able to change on her own.

Feeling more like herself, she insisted she was. Now,

she stared at the dress in the mirror. At the bruises blooming beneath the makeup. She peeled off the wig. Stripped away the armor. The performance.

And for a moment, she let herself feel it—the terror. The fury. The electricity still dancing through her limbs.

They weren't safe anymore. But maybe that was the point.

She hadn't come here to play it safe. She'd come to end this, and she'd do whatever it took to make sure she did.

SIX

Spence

THE APARTMENT WAS above a bakery that hadn't seen a health inspection since the Cold War. The scent of yeast and cinnamon clung to the furniture, but Spence barely registered it.

The safehouse apartment was sparse, featuring a sloped ceiling, a threadbare rug, and a kitchenette the size of a postage stamp—but secure. It was close quarters and did nothing for his restlessness, but it would hold, for now.

Spence kicked the door shut behind them and engaged the deadbolt. Three more locks followed, all of which were old-school. Manual. No digital footprint. The place was a dead zone—no Wi-Fi, no Bluetooth, no easy signals to trace. Just the way he wanted it. He could link to a secure Agency-approved satellite for what he needed, and no one could pick up on his extracurricular activities.

Jessie sank onto the worn striped couch without a word. Her eyes were glassy. That slap at the gala must have been brutal. Her ankle was swollen. She did her best to hide her limp, but he'd noticed it. He noticed everything about her.

They'd stopped at the hotel only long enough to change and grab their things. He set down his go-bag and crossed the room, kneeling in front of her. "Let me check you over."

"I'm fine." Her voice lacked conviction.

"You're limping, your face is bruised, and you haven't blinked in forty seconds. You're not fine."

She pushed against his shoulders and stood. "Spence—"

He didn't budge. "Sit down, shut your gob, and let me help, luv."

Something flickered in her eyes. She bit her tongue, but didn't move. "Gob?"

"Mouth."

"I know what it means. Just surprised you'd be so impolite when I'm injured."

He chuckled. "If you want impolite, I can use my street vernacular, which consists of plenty of curses and vulgarities, and you just said you were fine."

She winced. "You got me, okay? I'm not fine, but I will be. I don't need a nursemaid."

He angled her chin toward the light and examined her pupils. One was slightly more dilated. Just as he suspected, she had a mild concussion. "So I'm only good for wig detail and finding a safehouse?"

A one-shouldered shrug. "You have various uses."

In the bathroom, he rummaged through the cabinets and found a few first aid supplies. When he returned, she was still standing. Swaying, of course, but staying on her feet just for spite. So damned stubborn.

"Sit." He dropped the first aid stuff on the coffee table and pointed at the couch cushion. "I'm not asking. Do it, or I'll put you on your ass."

Jessie gave him the kind of look that had once made grown men rethink their careers. He didn't flinch. "Foot up."

With exaggerated exasperation, she muttered, "Fine," and herself with rigid control. As she lifted her leg, he sat on the coffee table and took it, bringing it to his lap.

He peeled off her shoe gently, his hands steady, but his pulse was going haywire. Her foot was bare inside the blue sneaker, her skin bruised and motled on the outside of the ankle. Her calf flexed under his touch, and she hissed.

"Breathe," he said, not sure if it was for her or him.

He pressed his thumb lightly along her ankle bone, gauging the damage. Jessie's mouth twitched. Another hiss escaped her sexy lips.

"Hurts?" he asked.

"No, feels great, Spence. Please do it again."

When he cocked a brow at her, she relented. "Only when you touch it like that." She'd still gone for derision, but her voice betrayed her, coming out too soft, almost erotic, to pull it off.

His gaze dropped to her lips. She cleared her throat. He dragged his attention from them, and their eyes locked. The moment suspended—quiet but volatile.

He didn't say a word. But he knew she felt it, too.

His own voice came out like his vocal cords had done a two-step with sandpaper. "Soft tissue injury. A strain." He wrapped a support bandage around it, not rushing, his fingers brushing against her skin with more care than he'd allow himself to admit. When he secured it, she left it in his lap. His cock was hard, and her eyes lingered on the bulge just inches from it under his zipper.

"That kiss at the gala," she said suddenly, eyes refocusing on his hands where he still held onto her foot. "Don't read into it."

Damn. Of course, she'd tackle the elephant in the room right now. And of course, it would be to shut down any possible feelings he had for her.

His jaw tightened with words he wouldn't allow himself to say. "Wouldn't dream of it."

She flinched, and he hated himself for saying it like that, but screw it. He had feelings for her. She knew it. He wasn't going to pretend otherwise.

He checked her over once more, then grabbed a cold pack from the freezer, adjusting his pants as he went. Returning, he handed it to her. "Put this on it. Keep your foot elevated. You need rest."

"What I need is to know who those men are, and what the hell they're building."

"That's my job. I'll figure it out."

Another flinch. He set his jaw and didn't let it get to him. She wanted him to be impersonal and stay on task? It was a load of tosh, but fine.

In the small, cramped corner filled with bookshelves and smelling of must, he powered up his laptop. It took ten minutes to establish a secure connection to a satellite, then he routed the data through ghost servers and encrypted lines.

While he waited for facial recognition to process the photos from the gala, he toyed with the vintage Queen Victoria shilling he carried with him. The silver edges had gone smooth from years of rubbing—habit, ritual, a tether. It was the only thing he'd kept from his mother after she shoved him out the front door at age eight with a busted lip and no coat. She'd handed him the coin like it meant something.

Maybe it had. Maybe it was her version of goodbye. All he knew was, he'd carried it every day, his whole life. It wasn't worth much, just like him. But it was all he had of that previous life before Ian Bastion, the mucker, had taken him off the London streets and become his mentor.

Another life. Another false identity. Another fucking trainwreck.

Spence rubbed a hand over his face and set down the coin, staring at it. Not tonight. He wasn't going down the rabbit hole now.

He picked up the shilling again, rubbing a thumb over the queen's face. Victoria was his sister's name, and

Spence had carried the damn coin into every part of his life. Every mission.

For Vicky. For him. For a life they'd never gotten to share.

A superstition? Sure. But also a promise. He still didn't know what had become of her after his mother's ex took Vicky away. And until he found her—until he fixed what had been broken—he wasn't losing this coin. Not ever.

His computer pinged, and there it was—the identity of the man who'd attacked Jessie. Darian Voss.

He dropped the name into a database, knowing it would trigger things on Langley's end. He'd been expecting a call from Flynn anyway. At least now, he might have something to tell him.

Minutes ticked by before the file revealed a plethora of intel. Voss wasn't just a muscle-bound brute—he was a former DARPA contractor with clearance higher than God and a specialty in AI-driven weapons systems.

Spence's gaze snagged on one section. Voss had been declared officially dead six months ago.

"Of course he's not dead," he muttered, clicking into another file. "No one ever stays dead anymore."

He froze for a second, listening to the sounds behind him. All he needed was for Jessie to have heard that off-the-cuff remark and get all up in his face about it.

But she didn't say anything. When he glanced over at the couch, he saw her stretched out on it, her arms hugging a pillow and her eyes at half-mast.

He let out a slow breath and went back to his digging.

Transaction logs linked Voss and Hastings to a front company headquartered near Görlitz—the exact location flagged by the CIA drop. The same compound that Voss and his friend had discussed at the gala—autonomous drones, facial recognition, and AI targeting protocols.

The pieces snapped together like a loaded weapon.

"J." He carried the laptop over to her, interrupting her half-dozing state. "I've got confirmation. The man who came after you is Darian Voss. He's helping Brewer weaponize the drones."

She sat up, blinking. Slowly, she shoved the pillow away and reached for the laptop. "At the Görlitz facility?"

He set the laptop in her hands to let her read the files. "Everything points to it. From what's in his dossier, I'd say it's a good bet that if Voss is involved, we're not talking about theoretical tech. Hastings and Brewer are planning for deployment on a massive scale."

Her jaw tightened as she scanned the files. Every few seconds, she blinked rapidly as if trying to bring the words into focus. "Then we go. Tonight."

"No," he said, sharply. "Not tonight. Not without more intel. That compound will be a fortress, and you're not going in there with a concussion and a rolled ankle."

Her eyes flared. "I'm not broken."

Broken. Her voice cracked on the word.

Why was everything a fight with her? He modulated his tone. "I didn't say you were, but I'm not letting you get killed because you're pissed off and rushing to get payback. Think it through. The payoff will be better."

She stood, grimaced, and quickly sat back down. "So what, we wait around? Bake some croissants while they ship out kill bots?"

Spence took back his laptop. "We do what we do best—recon. We pull surveillance from the area. We speak to our contacts here in Munich—Flynn and Del can obtain satellite passes, power grid layouts, and possibly even a roster of personnel at the site. We notify our team and create a plan. And then, we assume we'll need contingency plans, so we create a few of those, too."

"That will take days."

"Yes, and it assures we get Brewer and all of his assets. You've waited this long; you can wait a few more days. Our mission needs to be airtight. We can't let Brewer slip through our fingers this time." He looked at her and tried to see past the mask, past the fight. Tried to see the woman who'd nearly collapsed in his arms not two hours ago. "Do you trust me?"

She didn't break eye contact for once, but her pause made him squirm. Finally, when he thought she was going to eviscerate him, she sighed. "With my life."

He took a breath, then had her steal it.

"Just never with my heart."

The words landed like a sucker punch. He almost reeled backward. He wanted to slam his laptop down. To ask her what the hell she wanted from him.

Instead, he remained as impassive as the wall behind her. She could push him away all she wanted. He hadn't gotten this far in life by letting people trigger him. Even if she never gave him what he wanted—that very heart she didn't trust him with—he'd take what they had right now.

She watched him carefully. Trying to read his mind? When she couldn't see past his aloof expression, she mirrored it. "Three days. That's it. You have seventy-two hours and then, regardless of what Flynn says, with or without your help, I'm going to burn that place to the ground and rid the world of Harris Brewer."

Spence kept all emotion off his face. "Okay. Three days. It's a deal."

Her brows hiked up and her eyes widened. She hadn't expected him to agree with her.

He sat beside her, not too close, but close enough she could see his screen. He thought she might move, at least an inch or so, just because she was stubborn like that. She didn't, surprising him in turn.

The smell of bread and burnt coffee drifted up from below. Something about it reminded him of home. His mother. His sister.

He touched the coin in his pocket.

Outside, the sky over Munich was black and bottomless.

And somewhere east of them, in a fortified facility full of secrets and steel, Brewer was building a war.

SEVEN

Jessie

SHE HADN'T MEANT to fall asleep. Certainly not curled up on the sagging couch like some burned-out agent in a B-grade spy flick.

But after Spence all but ordered her to take the bedroom, she'd refused out of sheer principle, maybe because she didn't want to owe him. But also, because the idea of sleeping in a bed while he was only a room away felt too intimate. Too tempting. She didn't need that kind of vulnerability. Not tonight. Not with him.

Now, hours later, the blanket she'd yanked from the lumpy mattress was tangled around her legs, and her back ached like hell. Her ankle vied with it for her attention. The air still smelled like yeast, raspberries, and coffee, thanks to the bakery.

She pushed upright with a groan and limped to the kitchenette. The light was on in the tiny den next to it.

Spence.

Of course.

She found him exactly where she'd left him a few hours ago—at the old desk wedged between two bookshelves, eyes glued to the laptop screen. Fingers flying. A half-eaten protein bar beside the keyboard.

His shirt was unbuttoned, revealing his t-shirt, which sported a V, and his smooth, tan skin underneath. A thick layer of scruff dusted his jawline, and his hair stood at odd angles as if he had been raking his fingers through it.

She combed her fingers through her own hair, teasing out knots, and leaned on the doorframe. Words seemed to escape her. Before Hagar and Brewer, she'd been an ace at making small talk. Now? It was as if her brain no longer functioned that way.

She cleared her throat. "Did you, ah, sleep at all?"

He didn't glance her way. "Didn't want to waste the bandwidth."

"You're going to burn out your retinas."

"Already did. Back at university."

She rolled her eyes, but the corner of her mouth twitched. A little.

Spence glanced at her. Dark smudges had appeared under his eyes. The lines around his mouth seemed deeper, thanks to a scowl. She wasn't sure if it was for her or what he'd been reading.

His gaze raked over her body, assessing her messy hair, bruised cheek, and the swollen ankle she was favoring. She had the unnerving desire to straighten up and meet that assessment with defiance.

When he spoke, however, that rebellious feeling evaporated. "You didn't sleep much, either."

Funny, because it had been a deep sleep. Something she hadn't had in a very long time. No nightmares, no shakes. With Brewer back on the scene, she'd expected the worst ones to rear their heads.

They hadn't.

Not even her aches and pains had bothered her. She'd slept like the dead.

Was it due to the adrenaline from last night's encounter at the gala, or was it because of the man sitting across the room who made her feel safe?

She hadn't lied when she told him she trusted him with her life.

He was still studying her, and it made her uncomfortable. Her stomach growled, and she placed a hand over it as if that would silence it. "I can function just fine on three to four hours of shuteye. All I need is a shower and some coffee, and I'll be ready to go."

He shifted so he could angle the screen toward her, tapping a couple of keys to bring up what he wanted her to see. "Got a hit."

She crossed the room and leaned in, trying not to touch him. On one of the screens, she saw a series of pictures of young girls. Not just pictures—missing persons bulletins. Before she could ask about them, they vanished, thanks to his tapping fingers. In their place, a grainy black-and-white appeared. Security cam footage, timestamped six hours earlier. She squinted at it. "Is that the compound?"

"You bet your secret decoder ring it is. I managed to piggyback on a low-orbit satellite and tapped into a rural fiber-optic line feeding the Görlitz compound's surveillance network. It's only the exterior. Still working on gaining access to the internal feeds. If there are any access points. I'm doubtful about that."

What he'd captured, though. Her breath stuck in her throat, her blood going cold.

Hastings posing as Keller. And next to him—Harris Brewer.

Jessie's stomach clenched. Seeing him again made her whole body go rigid. The room spun for a second, and she had to grab the edge of the desk. *Breathe.*

She blinked. Once. Twice. But the image didn't change. She closed her eyes and focused on her aching ankle, her stinging shoulder. Pain always had a way of stopping the panic.

When she flipped open her lids again, she felt back in control. She sneered at the photo. "There you are, you bastard." Her words dripped with the disdain she felt in every cell. "No one's had eyes on you for six months, but we got you."

Spence leaned back, rubbing his eyes. "I assumed he'd had plastic surgery and changed his appearance so he could stay off our radar, but nope. Facial rec confirms it. This is him. Our guy is alive and well and definitely working with Keller, er, Hastings. The Pentagon security breach was most certainly him."

She'd known this day would come when Brewer was flesh and blood again. Not just a shadow. Not a ghost. He was back. Her body started down the panic highway, thanks to her PTSD, but she shut it down. In her mind, she painted a red bullseye on his chest.

Spence typed a series of commands, lines of code scrolling by in one of the black boxes. "If only I could worm my way inside the warehouse. Tap into some form of audio. There has to be a way to see and hear them. Without it, they're ghosts."

Her pulse kicked harder. Even ghosts left fingerprints. He just had to find them. "This is it, though. We need to get to that warehouse. Now, before the meeting is over."

Spence shook his head. "That photo is from two a.m. —and before you break my neck for not waking you, I didn't get into the feed until thirty minutes ago. This is from a recording. The meeting was probably hours ago. What we need are live feeds, terrain intel, and an exit plan—"

"Exit plan? Jesus, Spence, you sound like Meg and Dec. Everything has to be planned out. Everything has to be timed. Even if it was hours ago, Brewer might still be there. We need to find out." She checked the old-fashioned cuckoo clock hanging on the wall. "If we leave now, we can get there in the next hour."

He scoffed. "No."

That was it. One word.

Anger roared through her. She smacked the top of the desk. "That will be your live feed. That's how you get your terrain intel. We can form an *exit plan* after I gun Brewer down and send him to hell."

Spence stopped typing. He stood so abruptly, his dark eyes hardening into flint, that she had to stumble backward to keep him from bumping his chest into hers. "Enough with the renegade bullshit, Mendoza. Above everything else, you are still a CIA operative. You are tasked with a mission, and that mission has parameters." His voice was as stern as his eyes. "Those parameters are in place to protect you, me, and the rest of our team, as well as to catch the bad guys we pursue. I'm all for taking risks and bending a few rules, but your recklessness needs to stop right here, right now. You are not a vigilante." His voice lowered. A muscle jumped in his jaw. "I don't want to pull rank, but Flynn put me in charge. I will pull you off this mission and ship your reckless ass right back to Langley if you keep acting like this."

It was as if he'd slapped her. She lashed out before she could stop herself, storming across the room—well, as much as she could manage on her traitorous ankle—and grabbed the first thing she could find—a cracked ceramic vase sitting on top of an old wooden chest. She hurled it across the room at him. It missed and crashed against the wall, shattering it. "You don't understand!"

Spence didn't flinch. He crossed the space between them in two strides. Caught her wrist. Not hard, just enough to stop her from grabbing something else. Just enough to pull her in close.

She froze.

His breath mingled with hers. His eyes searched her

face. Fire and pain and something raw burned between them.

"Jess," he said, low.

She didn't pull away. Couldn't. She hated how much she wanted to lean into him. To let Brewer and everything else she'd been carrying all these months fall away.

Their lips were inches apart. Should she do it? Give in to these raging feelings that weren't only about her nightmares but about...him?

A crash came from downstairs.

Spence stepped back, releasing her. "You might be surprised at what I understand about the past and how it keeps a grip around your neck, no matter what you do."

Air. She needed air. Jessie turned without a word and limped toward the rusted fire escape. She shoved open the window, cool air slapping her face. She braced her hands on the railing, breathing hard.

Behind her, Spence followed.

Damn him.

But he didn't say anything. They stood in silence.

The city was still dark. The street below was empty except for a garbage truck rumbling past. Through the thin walls and wooden floorboards, more sounds came from the bakery as the owner prepared to open shop.

Spence blew out an audible breath. "Every time I get near you, I forget how to breathe. I forget what the mission even is."

"That's the problem." She stared out over the rooftops. The sunrise did little to scatter the heavy, gray clouds. Her voice cracked. "I never forget."

His body tensed. She could have bounced that silver coin he was constantly toying with off his tight muscles, straight back, clenched jaw.

She turned back toward the apartment. "I need a shower, and then that coffee."

He raised his face to stare at the sky, as if he couldn't stand to look at her. "I'll grab breakfast from downstairs. Don't overdo it. You need to keep that ankle elevated again today."

Embarrassment crept up the back of her neck and into her scalp. God, she was acting like one of those ridiculous drama queens on a reality show. She felt like a bomb about to explode every damn day. Hypervigilance. Fear. Her adrenals were shot. "Bossy bastard."

He smiled faintly, and her pulse kicked. "You love it."

It was just an offhanded remark, but of course, it wasn't. The truth was, she hated being bossed around, especially after her time with Brewer.

Yet, coming from Spence, it wasn't so bad.

And didn't that scare the shit out of her? The ugly truth was, she did love it. His attention. His protection.

Him.

No, no, no. She could never love anyone again. Ever. They would only end up being used against her.

And that was the real danger.

EIGHT

Spence

THE HOMEY SCENTS of vanilla and fresh bread clung to Spence's clothes as he returned to the apartment. The fight with Jessie had left him on edge.

He stuck the waxy bag of pastries under an arm and balanced a coffee tray as he unlocked the apartment door. At least the safehouse was still clean. No one had come after them here.

Yet.

He used a foot to nudge the door shut behind him. From the back of the small apartment came the faint sound of the shower running.

He paused.

For a split second, the image of Jessie behind that thin bathroom door hit him hard—water cascading down toned curves, hair slicked back, eyes closed, lips parted. He swore under his breath and shook it off, zeroing in on the small kitchenette. Coffee. Food. *Act normal.*

In the cramped space, Spence lined the pastries on the chipped counter like he was setting out a peace offering. He tried not to imagine what Jessie would look like walking into this scene. What *they* might look like, sitting across from each other at the table. Sharing breakfast like it was normal.

Like they were normal.

The faucet in the kitchenette dripped once, twice. He yanked it tighter. One cupboard stuck open no matter how many times he slammed it shut. He stared at it for a long second, jaw tight, then turned away.

Every piece of him wanted to knock on the bathroom door. Not for anything reckless—just to hear her voice. Make sure she was still here. Still safe.

He knew she was, but... Too many things were pretending to be okay.

She wasn't okay. He wasn't, either.

Not when all he could think about was the woman in the next room, wrapped in steam, and what it would feel like to join her.

Don't go there.

She was already too deep under his skin.

And damn, he wanted her to bury herself even deeper.

He took a seat at the small table. Checked the time. Got up and grabbed his laptop. It felt too weird, too rude, to eat without her, but he was restless, and if he couldn't stuff his face, he needed a distraction that would keep his mind off her.

Returning to the table, he resumed his seat. The screen blinked to life. He scanned the feeds—drone chatter, darknet threads, a few flagged updates from Flynn. Lines of code rolled down it like rain, and Spence welcomed the familiar rhythm. Data calmed him. People, not so much.

But it was the notification in his burner inbox that made his pulse skip a beat.

Subject line: Re: Looking for V.

Sender: 609_station

The burner email wasn't connected to the Agency. It was part of an underground network he'd built himself over the years to locate missing persons. It tracked girls who'd gone missing from foster care systems, shelters, hospitals—girls no one seemed to remember.

Spence's hands hovered over the keyboard before opening the message. His heart did the thing it always did when he thought maybe—just maybe—this time…

The message was short. A series of letters and numbers: *Vic609-bellcov-97firewatch.*

Not a phone number. Not an address. Nothing immediately recognizable. It might be a coded file path. Or an old username. Or a place—Bellcov? Firewatch?

He conducted a quick search, but neither name yielded anything significant. He copied the message into a separate doc, encrypted it, and sent a flag to one of his offline drives. It would have to wait.

Just like it always did.

Because right now, his 'missing' person wasn't a stranger from an online thread. She was the woman in the next room, with a bruised face and a heart she'd padlocked shut. A woman he could touch, but never reach.

The shower cut off. A second later, so did Spence's ability to think clearly.

He shoved the burner account out of view and closed the laptop's lid. The message would keep. For now.

Footsteps padded down the short hall. He grabbed his coffee and schooled his face like he hadn't just been obsessing over encrypted ghosts from his past—or Jessie.

She appeared, her hair damp and messy, a loose T-shirt skimming her hips, black leggings clinging to curves that did nothing to help him remain professional. A towel hung around her neck, and she was barefoot, her injured ankle clearly still tender as she walked.

His chest constricted.

She looked...better. Still bruised, but awake, alert, alive. Which should've settled something inside him.

It didn't.

"Smells like heaven in here," she said, fluffing her hair with the towel.

He covered the hitch in his breath with a smirk. "I figured coffee and carbs might distract you from throwing more pottery at my head."

Jessie let out a short laugh. "No promises."

She slid into the chair across from him, and for a moment, it almost felt normal. Two agents on a break. Coffee. Pastries. Shared silence.

But the way she devoured the cheese Danish was anything but normal.

He tried not to stare, but her lips were pink from the heat of the shower, and her eyes still held shadows from the night before. She looked like something from one of his better dreams—and he didn't have many of those.

His own croissant sat untouched.

"You're not eating," she said around a bite.

"I'm watching you annihilate a poor, defenseless pastry."

Her eyes narrowed. "This poor, defenseless pastry is the only reason I haven't strangled you yet."

He bit back a smile, but the sharp ache behind it lingered. "What did I do this time?"

She heaved a heavy sigh, sipped her coffee. "Nothing. You're being nice. Human. I just haven't had…"

"Normal, human interactions much lately?"

She pointed a finger at him and nodded. "Bingo. Bitch is my default setting these days. I'll… I'll do better."

The smile broke free. Something in his chest loosened. He picked up the croissant and enjoyed its buttery taste. So many things he wanted to say, but he knew this was a good moment to keep those comments to himself.

The silence between them thickened, charged, but not hostile.

Just…close.

She gave him a wry look, as if she knew it was killing him to hold back. To keep his mouth full of pastry so he didn't insert his foot into it. A crumb stuck to her bottom lip, and he reached out without thinking—then stopped himself.

Bad idea.

He jerked his hand back, grabbed his coffee as if that had been his plan all along. "Flynn wants an update. We've got a call with him in less than an hour."

Jessie wiped her mouth with the towel, then leaned back. "Figures. Can't let us go rogue for more than six hours without reeling us back in."

Spence offered a half-smile. "He's just trying to keep you from assassinating a high-value target without backup."

She shrugged. "Somebody's gotta do it."

He chuckled. A beat passed. Then another.

Jessie took another bite, then set down the pastry and picked up her coffee again. She didn't drink it right away. Instead, she let her gaze slide across the table—toward his closed laptop. "He's probably got eyes on us anyway." She paused, then added, "Not that I blame him."

A flicker of amusement crossed her face, but it didn't last. Her gaze lingered again—this time more deliberate. "I noticed something on your laptop last night."

He stiffened. "Is that so?"

"Missing persons. Is there someone you're searching for?"

He didn't answer. Couldn't for a long moment. "It's a side project. I promise it won't distract me from this mission."

Jessie waited. Gave him a moment. When he said

nothing, she continued, her voice gentler. "We all have those, don't we? Side projects?"

Spence's hand tightened around the last piece of croissant. The flaky bread turned to dust in his mouth. A long beat passed between them—tense, humming with the quiet knowledge that this was not just another offhand question.

He looked up and met her eyes.

She didn't press, didn't push. "You don't have to tell me, but if you ever want to talk about it, I'm here."

That damn lump clogged in his throat again. He hated it. Hated how easily she could reach the parts of him he buried.

For a second, the words trembled on the edge of his tongue. But if he opened the vault—if he let Victoria's name out into the room—it wouldn't just be about his sister anymore.

It would be about his *failure*.

His past.

All the ways he'd let her down.

He shoved back his chair, the legs screeching against the floor. "I need more coffee," he muttered, grabbing his cup and heading toward the counter. He'd have to brew a pot.

Jessie's voice followed him, quiet and calm. "Thanks."

He paused. Turned just enough to glance at her over his shoulder.

"For what?" he asked.

She joined him and began filling the carafe with water. "For taking care of me."

The words made him pause. Jessie Mendoza didn't say thank you for anything. She especially didn't thank people for caring about her.

She didn't allow people to care.

And still—she'd said it.

He stared at her long enough that she stopped what she was doing and stared back. "I didn't..." he started. But his voice cracked.

He abandoned the coffee maker and sat down again, slowly. The chair creaked under his weight. Jessie finished pouring the water in and getting it started. Then she joined him at the table as the smell of ground coffee filled the air.

His hand dipped into his pocket.

The coin was warm from his body heat. He turned it over in his fingers once. Twice.

Then, he looked at her and told her something he'd never told anyone. Not even his adopted brothers, who knew all the dirt, all the ugliness about him. "I'm looking for my baby sister."

NINE

Jessie

THE WAY SPENCE looked at the coin in his hand, like it held the weight of his entire past, made Jessie's throat tighten. She didn't speak, didn't move—just watched him turn it over, his jaw clenched, eyes far away.

I'm looking for my baby sister, he'd said.

It was the kind of sentence that had so much behind it, so much more story. But Spence wasn't one to embellish. He let it hang there, stark and raw, like an open wound he'd finally decided to show.

Jessie swallowed. The coin gleamed in the light, but it wasn't the silver that held her attention. It was the look in his eyes, the tone of his voice. There was something different there than she'd ever seen or heard before.

She wasn't sure, but it appeared that Spence Stirling,

the man who built firewalls for breakfast and brought terrorists to their knees with one swift kick, had just opened the door to a secret side of him.

For her.

For a moment, she didn't know if she wanted to thank him or run.

She opened her mouth—no idea what she would say —and the laptop chimed.

The soft sound managed to hit like a gunshot in the silence. Spence flinched. So did she. Whatever fragile thread had connected them snapped.

Spence was instantly back to his usual self, opening it and frowning at the screen. "It's Flynn."

"Already?" Jessie glanced at the kitchen clock, hurriedly whipping off the towel from around her neck and raking a hand through her wet hair. She joined Spence on his side of the table. "I thought we had—"

He was already clicking to answer. Director Flynn's lined face filled the screen, voice sharp with urgency before either of them could say a word. "We've got eyes on Brewer," Flynn said. "In Paris."

Jessie's heart stuttered. "What?"

Spence cocked his head, every inch of him going rigid. "That's not possible, mate. He was at the Görlitz compound less than four hours ago."

"Then he's either learned how to teleport," Flynn said, voice strained, "or he has doppelgängers."

Jessie leaned in. "You have photos? Video?"

"We do." The sound of Flynn's typing preceded a

traffic cam shot of Brewer crossing a street. "Del has confirmed it's legit."

It *did* look like Brewer, the bastard. Jessie's guts crawled. "It can't be unless he's cloned himself."

"She's right." Spence shared his screen and the security footage of Harris and Hastings outside the warehouse. "He's teamed up with Jonathan Hastings, a former CIA handler, who now goes by Jonas Keller."

Flynn grunted. "Hastings? Are you sure? You've located him after all this time? What the hell is he doing with Brewer?"

"He has an ax to grind with Langley, just like Brewer does," Jessie said. "And since I was one of his operatives, I can confirm it's him."

There was a string of cursing on the other end. "Brewer had amassed quite a team, then, hasn't he?" Another round of cursing and more pecking at a keyboard. "Del cross-checked the cam footage with his personal facial recognition. It's solid—CCTV in Paris caught Brewer outside the Galerie Vivienne just before sunrise. Here's another kicker—Meg swears she saw him in D.C. yesterday, outside the Naval Observatory. That's three cities in under twelve hours."

Spence's fingers curled into fists. "Then it's not him. At least not every time. He's using decoys, impersonators. High-quality masks, makeup, implants—whatever tech he can get his hands on. He's using them to muddy the waters."

Jessie paced. "So we're chasing ghosts and playing wack-a-mole."

"No." Spence's voice was confident. "One of those sightings is real. The rest is noise. And if I were Brewer, and I had something to launch—something I wanted no one to interfere with—I'd be at the launch site."

Flynn grunted. "Tell me about the warehouse."

Jessie started to give her report, but Spence spoke over her like a man reciting scripture, facts, and probabilities layered with terrifying potential. It annoyed her, and yet, she realized why he'd done it—he was in charge, whether she liked it or not, and giving Flynn their official update was his job, not hers.

"That warehouse," Spence continued, "could house hundreds of thousands of drones. He possesses the necessary capacity, AI technology, and infrastructure. If he activates that swarm, we're talking city-wide blackouts. Air traffic disruption. Biological payloads. EMP devices. Contamination of water supplies. There are no limits to what he could do."

Flynn rubbed a hand over his face. "Jesus."

Spence was grim. "We're looking at apocalypse-level damage."

The line went quiet. Jessie could practically hear the seconds ticking past in Flynn's head, weighing options, imagining political fallout, calculating the risks to innocents.

When he spoke again, his voice was low and measured. "You two stay in Germany. I want eyes on that compound. No breach. No heroics. Just confirmation. I can't put any plans into action until I have that. No breach," he repeated. "Got it, Mendoza?"

Jessie folded her arms. "You want confirmation, you'd better be ready for noise."

"Don't test me," Flynn snapped. "This is me trusting you not to get dead."

"My watchdog already has me on a leash," she fired back. At Spence's wince, guilt made her sigh and close her eyes for a split second. She'd just damaged the bond between them. Again. Shaking it off, she resumed pacing. "And if we get confirmation?"

"We go in hot and hard." Flynn's voice wavered—just for a second. "But I'm not gonna sugarcoat this. Brewer escaped on my watch. Six months have passed, and we haven't brought him in. The president's morning brief is in a few hours. If I don't give her something concrete, my head's on the block."

Spence frowned. "Flynn—"

"If I get yanked, Black Swan gets shut down. Best-case scenario, you're reassigned. Worst-case, they bury the whole program and throw us in a hole somewhere for treason and incompetence."

Jessie's pulse thudded. That couldn't happen, could it? She'd known this was high-stakes, but hearing it out loud like that was like staring down a sniper scope.

Brewer's photo disappeared, and Flynn looked straight into the camera. "If I'm removed, go off-grid. Immediately. Don't wait. Don't call Langley. Don't trust anyone."

Spence nodded, grave. "Understood."

Jessie gawked. How could he be so cool about this?

"That's not going to happen, sir. They won't remove you. You're the GOAT."

Flynn snorted. "One more thing. If they do take me out, if this is my last call with you—don't stop. Don't let that bastard disappear again. Find Brewer. Stop him. End it."

Jessie gripped the edge of the table. How could this be happening? *Damn Brewer*. He'd already taken so much from all of them.

She couldn't believe they were having this conversation, and yet, everything Brewer touched, he corrupted. Flynn was the most loyal, hard-working spy around. His commitment to his country was unmatched. She could only hope to live up to his standards someday. She firmed her voice. "You have my word."

Flynn blinked, then nodded once. The screen went black.

The silence afterward was heavy and absolute.

Jessie's eyes locked on Spence's. "We can't screw this up."

He pocketed the coin. Shoved the chair back to rise. "We won't."

He said it like a promise. Somewhere east of them, in a steel compound full of death and code, Brewer was planning the end of everything. They couldn't afford failure—not now. Not ever. The swans were the only thing standing in his way.

Jessie turned to stare out the narrow window above the sink. "You ever wonder what we'd be doing if we weren't chasing terrorists and megalomaniacs?"

Spence didn't answer right away, staring at the blank screen. She knew he was thinking of his sister. "Yeah," he said. "But then I remember why we do it—to stop them and keep our loved ones safe. For me, there's no higher purpose."

TEN

Spence

THE WORLD WAS ABOUT to burn, and it was up to him to stop it.

Jessie returned to the table, swiping their half-eaten breakfast aside. "We need to go. Now. Get eyes on that warehouse—"

He cut her off. "What if it's a trap?"

She froze, like someone had yanked a wire inside her. Her brow tightened. "You think Brewer knows we're watching?"

He pushed back from the table and stood. "I think it's exactly the kind of game he plays. You know him better than almost anyone, including Tessa. Is this real, or is he feeding us just enough to get us moving? To make us expose ourselves?"

She didn't answer right away. Her jaw shifted, her

fingers flexed, and she glanced at the doorway. That alone told him everything.

"He's done it before," Spence said, contemplating how to wrap his mind around all the ways Brewer could screw them. "Sent up a flare one place—hit the real target somewhere else."

Jessie stared toward the window, toward something Spence couldn't see. Maybe a memory. Maybe her own guilt. Her silence said more than any confirmation.

"Tessa never saw it coming," he added. "None of us did. He's led us on a royal goatfuck for over a year, starting with your and Meg's abduction by Hagar."

Jessie dragged in a breath through her nose. Those memories still had to trigger her, even now. Her voice was lower when she spoke again. "He's always five steps ahead. Always watching the board from above, like he's playing chess while we're monkeying with checkers."

She brought her gaze to his, tension bleeding from her shoulders. Her fight hadn't disappeared; it had only shifted. Focus was clear in her eyes. "You're right," she said. "We need a plan."

Spence didn't let her change of heart slow him down. The moment Jessie gave that rare, quiet agreement, he was moving—fingers on the keyboard, pulling up encrypted files, spinning through images Del had tagged from the Görlitz compound.

"First things first," he said. "We need gear. NVGs, comms, drones, thermals, surveillance cams, trackers. If we're gonna play in his sandbox, I want to bring our own toys."

Seemingly unable to sit still, Jessie jumped up and came around to watch him work. "And you know where to get all that?"

He gave a dry smile. "I know a guy."

"Of course you do. You always know a guy."

She didn't ask questions, though, and that told him just how much her trust in the mission—and maybe him —was shifting.

"We might be on stakeout for hours or days. There's no way to predict. I want the layout memorized. Entry points, blind spots, natural cover, possible sniper nests. We can't just eyeball it from a hilltop."

Jessie exhaled, clearly tamping down her instincts to move fast. "I assume you want to map exits, too."

"Multiple," he confirmed. "Worst case? We get spotted. We need more than one way out. A van, two bikes, fake plates, burner phones, backup IDs—"

"Jesus, Spence."

He paused to glance up at her. "This is Brewer. If he's laying a trap, we can't play this loose."

She tilted her head, studied him. "How soon do you think before he launches the drones?"

Spence didn't have a solid answer. He clicked open a map file, dropping a few new pins along the border of Görlitz's industrial zone. "No idea, but if he activates them before we're ready..." His insides churned. "We don't get a second chance."

Jessie moved closer to look over his shoulder. "All this stuff... this isn't just about doing recon for more than a few hours. You're equipping us in case we do need to go in and dismantle the drones."

"That's one of the contingency plans we need to prepare for."

He reached for the manila envelope tucked into his go-bag—the one from their contact in the park. Inside was a satellite printout of the compound perimeter, hand-marked with vantage points and drainage tunnels.

"Asset said this ridge has a solid line of sight." He pointed it out to her. "But we'll need cover. Camouflage tarps, maybe a heat-dampening tent. Nights are cold, and I don't want us lighting anything to stay warm."

Jessie's brow furrowed. "This isn't recon. It's war prep."

Was it? Was he being over the top with this because he was so damned determined to keep her safe? He nodded once. "It's how I work."

She stared at the map, jaw tight, her energy coiling beneath the surface. Spence snapped the map shut and grabbed his phone.

Jessie raised a brow. "You calling your drone guy?"

He shook his head. "This is deeper. We'll need gear that Langley won't authorize. And I'm not filing a request through backchannels that Brewer's spies might intercept. We don't have time for it anyway."

He scrolled through a string of burner numbers and hit one labeled only with a spade emoji.

"You trust this guy?" Jessie asked, skeptical.

"No," Spence said, tone flat. "But I trust his prices."

It rang once.

Twice.

Then a mechanical voice, disguising the real one, said, "It's been a while, you mucker."

Spence exhaled. Still alive. Still dealing. Code name Bellringer sounded like his usual self—cold, clipped, always three breaths from a threat. Their history went back to Bucharest, to a mission that ended with too many bodies and not enough truth. Spence still remembered the look in the man's eyes when he realized who'd sold him out. He hadn't forgotten. Spence doubted he ever would. They'd never exchanged real names, just burner numbers and blood-soaked favors.

Trust didn't factor in.

But reliability? That, the bastard had in spades, hence the emoji. Spence kept his tone neutral. "Need eyes in the dark. Two-person op. Gear list incoming."

A pause as if he was checking something—his watch, a calendar, his latest reality TV show? "Half an hour. Where the bells never ring."

The line went dead.

Jessie folded her arms. "You want to tell me what the hell that means?"

He met her eyes. "It means keep your weapon close and don't ask questions you don't want answers to."

She snorted. "You're such a romantic."

But her smirk didn't last long. Spence started typing the list to Bellringer: *NVGs, mini drones, encrypted comms, EMP scramblers, tactical vests, two .45s with suppressors, spare mags, untraceable SIM cards.*

He hesitated. Then added: *counter-surveillance gear.*

Because if this *was* a trap, Brewer would already be watching. He couldn't take chances. Couldn't get caught with his bloody knickers down.

Jessie watched him quietly and apparently didn't miss how his fingers hesitated over the keys. "What aren't you telling me?"

Spence didn't look up. "Don't know what you mean, luv."

"About all of this? You're always overanalyzing and overpreparing, but this seems like something more. What is it? What's eating you?"

Should he tell her? No. He used to believe in what he built. He used to think he could out-code the world's problems. Now? That warehouse outside Görlitz was full of his ghosts. His biggest failure. "I'm focused on what we need to do, that's all."

Jessie went back to studying the map in silence. It was enough.

"Let's go," he said finally. "The meet's across town, and I don't want to miss our window."

She grabbed her jacket. "You sure he'll show?"

"He's scared of me," Spence said. "He'll show."

Outside, the streets were damp from an early drizzle, gray clouds hanging low and heavy. The city was waking up, but their world felt like it was closing in on them.

As they reached the curb, Jessie glanced over at him. "You really think Flynn's gonna get axed over this?"

Spence hesitated, then gave a single, grim nod. "I think everything's about to blow. And we need to be ready when it does."

ELEVEN

Jessie

THE MEETING POINT looked like the kind of place people went to vanish.

Under pouring rain, thanks to the storm system moving through the area, a half-collapsed loading dock slouched behind a wall of stacked shipping containers, graffiti bleeding across the rusted steel. A single overhead bulb flickered and buzzed, casting strobe shadows across the cracked asphalt.

Jessie scanned the perimeter from the rental car, every nerve on edge as her nose picked up fumes of oil under the scent of rain. "Too many entry points. Too easy to bottleneck us."

Spence shifted in the driver's seat, calm in that unnerving way of his. He hadn't spoken much—just drove them out here like a man on rails, locked in his head and scanning the digital map in his mind. "He won't bottleneck us," he said. "If he's going to screw us, he'll drive a truck straight through and detonate it."

"Comforting." Her hand went to her waist to check her sidearm before she remembered she wasn't carrying.

And didn't that make her feel even more like a sitting duck?

This meetup wasn't just about buying gear, and it wasn't a simple dead drop with a street-level asset. This was black market territory. An appointment with someone who didn't give a damn about CIA credentials or mission parameters.

Jessie held onto the door handle. Her gaze snapped to every movement in the shadows around the hulking warehouse. A dog barked in the distance, and once in a while, she heard engine noises from the highway.

Her fingers drummed on the handle in time with the rain. It wasn't only this setup that had her skin prickling. It was Washington.

Flynn's warning replayed in her skull on a loop. If he went down, Black Swan went with him. If the division fell, so did every operation they'd worked on. Every life they'd saved. Every file they'd buried and every enemy they'd arrested.

They'd become fugitives overnight. Not soldiers. Not operatives.

Ghosts.

Ironic, that. Part of their off-the-books description was *to be ghosts*. To stay in the shadows so the world didn't know who they were or what they did to protect their country.

The worst part? If the Black Swan Division were terminated, Brewer would win.

She couldn't—*wouldn't*—let that happen. She mentally repeated her promise to Flynn as she checked her watch. It was still early in D.C., but the president and her advisors would call their morning meeting soon, if they hadn't already. "You think he's already gone? Flynn?"

Spence didn't answer immediately. The sound of a diesel engine growled in the distance, growing louder. "He'll fight until they drag him out by his badge." He glanced at her, voice like cut stone. "Deputy Director Stone and Director Allen will fight to save him. I want to believe he'll survive this morning's meeting and still be standing, but let's be prepared for the worst-case scenario. From here on out, until we hear differently, we act like we're on our own."

A van appeared without headlights, its matte black body gliding into view like a predator emerging from the gray mist. No plates. No markings. Just a shadow with wheels.

Jessie gripped the handle tighter. "Tell me again that this guy doesn't kill his clients after they pay."

Spence didn't smile. "He only kills the ones who lie." He cut the car engine. "And I did betray him once, so stay alert."

"You what?" She flicked a glance his way and caught

his wink. Was he kidding? She wasn't sure. "Okay, good to know."

The van stopped twenty feet ahead under an overhang for deliveries that no longer came. "Come on," Spence said, exiting the car.

Jessie opened her door with care. Stepped out. Her boots crunched on broken glass.

Every instinct screamed *ambush*, but she walked forward anyway, ignoring the drenching she was getting, only because Spence was at her side.

If Flynn was out, if Langley turned its back on them, if Black Swan collapsed in the fallout—they'd have only each other.

The van's side door screeched open like the gates of hell. A man exited. He was late forties, maybe early fifties, and moved with uncanny grace—rigid spine, squared shoulders, every step economical and silent. She inventoried him from head to toe. Combat boots. Weathered cargo jacket. Glock holstered at his side, and a KA-BAR strapped to his thigh that told Jessie this guy didn't rely on bullets.

Beneath his untamed hair and a thick beard, his eyes were stone. No shine. No warmth. Just a cold, calculating void that said he'd been through enough wars—official and otherwise—that nothing surprised him anymore.

This was Bellringer.

He locked eyes with Spence and nodded once. Not a greeting, just... acknowledgement. "Still breathing," he said flatly.

Spence didn't blink. "You're harder to kill than most fungus."

"Fungi don't hold grudges."

"No," Spence said. "But they do spread."

Jessie stood motionless at Spence's flank. Bellringer's eyes drifted her way—sharp and assessing. She recognized the flicker of calculation: range, reflexes, threat level.

She returned the look with one of her own.

He raised a brow at Spence. "Brought your plus one with you. Cute."

Jessie tilted her head, all casual like. "I'm the one with the kill shot."

A twitch of something like amusement curved his mouth, though it never reached his eyes that stayed locked on Spence. "Still going for dangerous women, eh, man?"

Spence didn't rise to the bait. He stood there, arms loose at his sides, still seemingly as cocky and confident as the Great Conrad Flynn himself.

Jessie felt it, though—the tension beneath the banter. Bellringer wasn't an ally. He was a weapon they were borrowing. One with its safety off.

Bellringer gestured toward the back of the van. "Let's get this over with before I start to like you again."

He yanked open the rear doors. Inside was a black market fantasyland—every inch crammed with gear you couldn't find in any sanctioned agency locker. Drones the size of hummingbirds. Disassembled rifles with illegal mods. Surveillance bugs so small Jessie had to squint. Military-grade comms. Infrared goggles. EMP patches. A case containing encrypted burner phones that appeared to have just arrived from a darknet shipment.

Jessie stepped closer, careful not to show the awe that tugged at her. Her face remained neutral, unreadable, but inside, she cataloged it all. The sheer range. The caliber. The fact that Bellringer had the audacity to roll up to a drop site with this kind of firepower and not blink.

Spence moved like he'd done this dance a dozen times. He didn't hesitate, didn't posture. He just started checking items off a mental list in his head while speaking in low-code phrases. "Crows nesting by the third rail." "Flashbangs are too spicy." "Need eyes that see past dawn."

Bellringer kept up. No explanations. No translations. It was a language of war, whispered across foreign soil and blood-soaked history. He already had two bags filled with the gear Spence had requested in his text. Now, Spence was shopping.

Jessie crossed her arms and watched, alert. She didn't like being on the outside of a conversation—especially one this precise—but what could she do? Sure, she'd dipped her toes into the black market world plenty of times on ops, but this was a whole other level. This was *their* world.

Bellringer's gaze slid her way again. "You let her carry the payload?"

Jessie smiled. "You worried about me? Now, who's being cute?"

Spence examined a rifle. "Better watch your balls. She's tougher than both of us."

Bellringer chuckled. His dead eyes roamed over her, calculating. "From the looks of things, you'd better watch yours. What your dick wants is poor strategy. She might be worth it, but the fallout"—he made a whistling noise that sounded like a bomb falling to the ground—"... deadly."

Pig. Jessie wanted to flip him off. Instead, she winked. "I'm always worth it, and I'm his ace in the hole, not the bomb that's going to blow up in his face."

She hoped that was true.

A grunt, dismissing her. "Still betting on instincts over strategy?" he said to Spence.

Spence froze in mid-inspection of a scope for the rifle. Looked up slowly. "Still blaming me for what happened in Bucharest?"

Silence fell like a line drawn in the sand.

Jessie didn't breathe.

Bellringer's jaw ticked. "Some mistakes don't bury easily."

Spence didn't reply. He finished checking the scope, slid it into a pack, and zipped it shut like the conversation was over.

Jessie said nothing, but her pulse quickened. She filed it away. Bucharest. Something there had gone wrong. The betrayal Bellringer hadn't forgiven.

Spence is more dangerous than I thought.

A glance at his profile reassured her. He'd already shaken off Bellringer's unspoken threat, his demeanor sliding back to the calm, confident partner he always conveyed. It wasn't just an act—not like hers was. He'd survived shit that had given him that edge. He'd broken rules and made impossible choices that he carried around with him every day, masking them under humor and snark. Sure, she had, too, but in much different ways.

Bellringer tossed her a collapsible rifle. "For you, sweetheart. On the house."

She caught it and saw Spence's eyes harden. *Interesting.*

She grabbed one of the packs. It had to weigh as much as she did. Her ankle barked, and she shifted her stance, trying to act stronger than she was. "We done here?"

Bellringer's smile finally reached his eyes, but it was menacing. He saw right through her act. "If you say so, sweetheart."

Spence paid, and they loaded the gear in silence, both of them moving with purpose. Spence slammed the trunk shut, gave the alley a last sweep, then climbed behind the wheel. Bellringer pulled out without looking back.

Jessie dropped into the passenger seat, situating a new Ruger into an equally new holster around her waist.

The rain had slowed—soft, steady, tapping the windshield like a metronome counting down something neither of them wanted to face.

They pulled away from the meeting point, the car's tires slick against the damp pavement. Jessie kept her eyes on the blurred city lights as they slid past the window. But after a minute, she had to ask. "Bucharest?"

Spence's knuckles tightened on the wheel. "Botched extraction," he said finally. "My intel got his asset killed, and then I had to give him up, or my asset was going to die." Between the lines, with Bellringer's accusation and interest in her being Spence's 'plus one', she knew it had been a woman. A woman Spence must have cared about. Jealousy surged in her chest. "We didn't exactly toast champagne afterward."

Jessie turned to look at him. "That was before Langley?"

"Yep. Still working for the Queen, then, luv."

"How *did* you end up at Langley?"

A muscle twitched in his jaw. "MI6 gave me my walking papers after that incident. They trusted the code I wrote, but they no longer trusted me. The Agency came sniffing around."

They trusted the code I wrote, but they no longer trusted me. The words bothered her. She understood that kind of separation, but Spence's loyalty had always seemed part of his internal code, and doing what he had to do to keep an asset safe was mission-critical for most operatives.

"MI5 was stupid."

He shrugged it off. "The CIA would have done the same thing. They need our skills, but that doesn't mean they give a damn about the person behind them."

Another bomb that didn't sit well with her. It was true, though, wasn't it? The only reason she'd been cleared by those in the hallowed halls of Langley was because she was the ace in the hole for finding Brewer.

They drove another few blocks before she spoke again. This time, her voice was quieter. "So how'd you end up a Swan?"

Spence's fingers drummed the steering wheel. He gave a quirky smile that did nothing to convince her he wasn't still thinking about Bucharest. The asset. MI6. "That's classified."

Jessie snorted, playing along. All that was water under the bridge. She needed him to believe it made no difference to her. "Of course it is."

He glanced at her, the barest flicker of something behind his eyes. Regret? Warning?

She waited for him to speak again, but he didn't. She leaned her head back against the seat, the rain still whispering against the glass. The space between them—not the physical, but the emotional—wasn't warm, but it wasn't cold either.

It was shifting. Into what, she wasn't sure.

She rubbed her eyes. Perhaps it was simply the fluidity that came with working closely with a partner. She'd forgotten what that felt like. Had thought she didn't want or need it anymore. That she was better off on her own, doing things her way.

Now, she wasn't so sure.

TWELVE

Spence
  An hour later

THE RAIN HAD SOFTENED to a whisper, threading down the windshield, much like the nervous sweat trailing along his spine. A gray veil hung over the old industrial zone below, transforming the warehouse compound into a ghostly landscape of concrete and shadow.

From their perch on a crumbling overlook road—half hidden by brambles and forgotten fencing—Spence could just make out the dull glint of floodlights above the eastern loading dock.

He adjusted the laptop's angle on his knees, then switched between the drone feeds. Still nothing. Static. The occasional gust of wind rattled a piece of rusted signage somewhere down the hill, but the compound itself remained locked in stillness. A sleeping beast.

Jessie sat beside him in the passenger seat, watching the same nothingness through a pair of binoculars through her half-opened window. She hadn't spoken in twenty minutes. Which, for her, was restraint.

He exhaled, slowly and quietly. His fingers hovered over the keyboard, but his mind wasn't on the screen anymore.

It was on contingency plans.

Not for the drones.

For *her*.

If this was a trap—if Brewer was playing the kind of game Spence feared—then Jessie was the real target. She always had been. Brewer loved leverage, and nothing got under a person's skin faster than someone they couldn't save.

He'd studied Brewer's psychological profile and seen it in his own rearview mirror more times than he cared to count.

If things went sideways—if hell cracked open tonight —Spence had two escape plans mapped out. One along the old train route that veered south toward Czechia. Another through the forest trails, using gear Bellringer had provided to scramble heat signatures and jam tracking.

But both routes only worked if Jessie listened to him. If she didn't rush in headfirst like she always did.

He glanced sideways at her. Damp wisps of hair clung to her cheekbone, and her mouth was drawn tight in that focused, bulletproof expression she wore like armor.

God help him, he was starting to see cracks in it.

And that scared him more than the drones.

He tapped a key. Zoomed in. Nothing but two parked trucks and a stack of empty shipping pallets near the side entrance.

Low activity, high defenses. The worst kind of combination.

"You see anything?" she asked, finally breaking the silence.

He shook his head. "Not yet. You?"

She lowered the binoculars. "Just a looming headache on the horizon."

Spence leaned back in the seat. He didn't say it out loud, but it circled his thoughts like a shark... *If this is a trap, I need to be the one who walks in first.*

Because he'd failed once before.

And he wouldn't let history repeat itself.

Another twenty minutes went by. His muscles ached from stillness. From the anticipation that never quite exploded. He closed the laptop and rubbed his eyes before he took a few swigs from the thermos they shared.

Jessie was still watching the compound, but out of the corner of her eye, she was watching him, too. She'd noticed the laptop closing. The way his fingers hovered, then curled. The way he didn't quite settle. She finally said it. "You're exceptionally quiet."

The air was humid, and the rental stank like gun oil now. "Just focused."

"Bullshit," she countered calmly. As if she already knew what was really going on.

He let the silence stretch for a moment, debating saying what was on his mind. "It's strange."

"What is?"

"This." He motioned vaguely at the laptop, the van, and the gray German sky, bleeding into twilight. "I used to think the world made more sense behind a screen. Algorithms don't lie. Code doesn't stab you in the back. And if something breaks, you can fix it."

Jessie didn't comment, just listened and nodded. That alone made it easier to keep talking.

"People aren't like that," he continued. "They short-circuit. They ghost you. They change the rules mid-mission."

A brow lifted. "What is this about?"

He shook his head. What was he trying to say? "I'm too much in my head right now, thinking about Brewer and his traps. The past with Bellringer. My manipulative, lying adopted father. Hell, even the situation with Flynn. People let you down, betray you, trick you."

"You're saying you trust machines more than people?"

He considered it. "I'm saying code is easier. Cleaner. Less likely to disappoint you."

Jessie sighed, placing her hand on the console and toying with the cup holder. "Except when it gets hijacked by psychopaths and turned into drone armies."

He smiled. Briefly. "Fair."

The air was heavier now—not just with the weather,

but with the weight of what wasn't being said. "I spent a long time thinking if I stayed behind my personal firewall —kept my distance—I'd be safe," he murmured. "Detached. Efficient. Invaluable. But eventually..."

She set the binoculars in her lap. "Eventually, what?"

"It starts to feel like you're not even human anymore. Just part of the machine."

Jessie shifted in her seat to face him fully. "Is that why you signed on with the Swans?"

He hesitated. Not because he didn't know the answer —but because he did. "I thought if I were in the field again, I could stop hiding behind the tech. Be something real. Make it count."

Her voice was quieter now. "Did it work?"

Spence looked at her. Right at her. "I don't know yet."

For a moment, Jessie said nothing. The rain blurred the world outside into streaks and shadows. Then her hand, resting on the console between them, edged an inch closer.

She didn't touch him.

But she didn't have to.

The way she looked at him—steady, unflinching— made it harder to hide behind sarcasm or strategy. She leaned a little closer, still not touching. Just close enough that the warmth of her presence scraped against the colder parts of him.

"I never had any siblings," she said. "Losing your sister must have been hard."

His throat got tight. It was so like her to go right for

the jugular, realizing his armor was more about Victoria than any betrayal since. "She was five. Smart. Funny. Obsessed with birds. She used to call pigeons 'air rats,' but she'd feed them anyway."

A faint smile ghosted across her lips, gone as quickly as it came. "What was her name?"

He pulled out the coin, flipped it over. "Victoria. I called her Vic. Our mother was...broken. Drank more than she ate. We never had heat in winter. Barely had food." He swallowed. "She told me one night to get out. Said she couldn't afford both of us."

Jessie's jaw tightened, but she didn't interrupt.

"I was eight. I didn't think she meant it, but she did. Slammed me into the doorframe, she was so determined to shove me out. I curled up in the alley that night, didn't even have a coat. I looked for a way back in, but couldn't find one. The next day, the doors were locked, the curtains drawn. She acted like she didn't know me. Like I was some junkie begging on the steps."

His hands curled around the steering wheel, needing something to hold onto.

"God, Spence." Jessie's voice was quiet like the rain. "That's horrible."

He stared at the blurry bulk of the warehouse. Saw his childhood walk-up instead. "I started watching the place. Figured I'd wait her out. Then this guy showed up. One of her old boyfriends. Real piece of work. He knocked, she let him in. Twenty minutes later, he walked out with Victoria."

Jessie's fingers twitched on the console. Still not

touching him, but still giving him her undivided attention.

"She wasn't crying," Spence added, voice fraying at the edges. "She was holding his hand. Looking up at him like he was...safe." His breath hitched. "Like maybe she thought he was her new dad or something."

"What did you do?"

"I ran after them. Tried to stop him. He shoved me into the gutter, Vic screaming my name. He tossed her into the back of his car and drove off. I can still see her in that back window, hands pressed against her as she cried for me."

Spence blinked hard to fight the sharp sting of tears. God, how he'd failed her.

Jessie's voice was both compassionate and outraged. "That bastard." She finally touched him. "You've been looking for her ever since."

Her touch did things to him. Her compassion, too.

He peeled his hands off the steering wheel, wishing he could put them on that guy and choke him to death. Instead, he grabbed the thermos and passed it to her just to focus on something else, ignoring how his hand was shaking.

Their fingers brushed. He won the war on his emotions and slid that solid shield back into place. "I went to the cops, and they laughed at me. An eight-year-old, claiming his mum kicked him out and sold her five-year-old daughter to her ex. I didn't have his full name. No license plate. You get the picture. No one cared. No one looked. They didn't take it seriously, and a case was never even opened—I checked later on when I hacked into their database. She was just another missing girl from the wrong side of town."

Jessie took a swig from the thermos and screwed the cap back on, slowly, deliberately. Once done, she reached for him, gently placing her hand on his.

He held himself still, focusing on the contact. He would not allow himself to move or breathe wrong and break the moment. "After that, I stopped trusting people to do the right thing. Started building systems. Networks. Traps. I thought—if I could build something smart enough...maybe I'd never lose anyone again."

Her grip tightened.

He didn't pull away.

The spark that passed between them felt like a live wire.

That single touch did more damage than a bullet. It wrecked him. Undid something deep inside him that he'd welded shut.

"If she's out there," Jessie said, "we'll find her."

He turned toward her. "We?"

Their eyes locked. And for a moment, neither of them breathed. The space between them was almost nothing.

"Yes, we." She leaned in even more, determination burning in her eyes. "After this, our mission is Victoria. You and me. You may excel at computers and coding, and you may even be a damn good spy, but I do have certain skills and resources that can help." Her fingers lifted to stroke the side of his face. "And as you've been trying to prove to me, teamwork is crucial to a successful outcome of any mission."

If she moved even a fraction closer, I'd kiss her—and then everything would unravel.

Her gaze dropped to his lips, and he thought she might kiss him instead. Yet, she held him there, in that suspended moment, and that restraint nearly killed him more than a kiss would have.

He cleared his throat. Forced himself to look away. "We should—uh—swap shifts. You need rest."

"I'm not tired," she said, voice just as wrecked as his.

Spence forced himself to pull away from her touch before the gravity of it pulled him straight into something they couldn't afford.

He traded his laptop for his tablet and focused on the screen, heart still hammering. "I'll cycle through the feeds again. Make sure we didn't miss anything."

Jessie nodded, but her eyes lingered.

They worked in silence for a few minutes. Shadows lengthened. The warehouse remained a black silhouette against a bruised sky, quiet and unassuming—too quiet. Spence hated that. Stillness always meant something was coming.

The burner phone in his jacket vibrated. He stiffened, yanked it out, and checked the screen. "Fuck."

Jessie leaned over to look. "Who is it?"

Spence answered before the second buzz and hit the speaker button. "Go."

Declan Reid didn't waste time. "It's about our boss."

Every muscle in Spence's body went rigid. Jessie straightened, flicking a fearful gaze at him.

"What about him?" Spence asked, already bracing for impact.

"He didn't show up for the morning brief."

Jessie let out a gasp. "*What?*"

Spence's stomach turned. "Maybe he was delayed."

"That man who lives in fifteen-minute blocks? If he was going to be late, he'd have sent a coded message, three contingencies, and a backup voice memo. Nobody's heard from him since his call to you. You know anything about this little disappearing act?"

Spence swallowed hard. "I assume you've checked every crevice and corner inside Langley?"

"The place is locked down tighter than a vault, and Stone is crawling up every one of our asses. The majority are pretending it's business as usual, but we both know what that means."

Jessie shook her head and rubbed a hand over her face. "Either he's gone dark side or someone got to him. Jesus, please tell me you don't think he's dead or being flown to some foreign black site."

Declan grunted. "I don't think either. What I do think is that he's coming your way. Meg and I are flying dark right now, but she's making arrangements for us to do the same. Off the books, of course. Tessa's digging through chatter there in Western Europe, and she and Tommy are also on their way from Prague to converge with all of us in Munich. One thing's clear—we're behind more than one eight ball."

Jessie met Spence's gaze again. No more flirting. No more shared silences or maybe-later glances. Just the cold rush of truth settling between them.

"Keep your head down," Declan said. "If Flynn didn't disappear on purpose to help us out, that means someone has silenced him. Someone high up in the ranks. And that means, it's open season on all of us."

The line went dead.

Spence stared at the screen until it dimmed. The shadows outside had deepened, bleeding toward night.

Beside him, Jessie whispered, "Shit."

Yeah.

That about covered it.

THIRTEEN

Jessie

HER PULSE WOULDN'T SLOW down.

Not from the near kiss. Not from Flynn's ominous vanishing act.

The heat from Spence's body lingered beside her, a whisper of what almost happened. And in the space between breaths, the mission came crashing back. The warheads weren't nuclear, but they were just as dangerous—code and hardware instead of bombs and bullets.

Jessie pressed her palms against her thighs, staring out at the warehouse through the streaked windshield.

Flynn was gone. And if what Declan said was true, the political noose was tightening. They were officially in the dark. Off-book. Probably already considered rogue.

She took a shaky breath. While they'd considered this might happen, she still felt caught off guard. She wanted —*needed*—a plan. Her anxiety and PTSD were spiking hard. "What do we do, Spence? Please tell me you have that Plan B ready."

Spence's jaw was tight, his eyes fixed on the compound like he could will it to reveal something. When he finally spoke, his voice was just as tight as his jaw. "Same thing we were going to do before. Our mission hasn't changed."

Jessie nodded once. She needed that—the mission. Focus. She could unravel later. After Brewer was behind bars. Then, she could take an extended vacation in a warm spot and try to put everything behind her.

Everything except the man beside her. Her partner.

She adjusted the comms rig on her lap and slowed her breathing. Her adrenaline spiked—but this time, it was clean. Sharp. The kind that told her something big was about to happen.

And it wasn't about drones or their MIA boss.

Something had shifted between her and Spence.

She didn't know what scared her more.

Movement at the gate caught her attention. Both her and Spence's gazes snapped toward it as a dark SUV and a panel truck rumbled into view, headlights off. They rolled past the entrance checkpoint like they owned the place—no stops, no questions. That alone told her what she needed to know. "We've got company."

Spence was already moving. He powered up the

signal interceptor and adjusted the satellite link, fingers flying across his tablet like a pianist mid-performance.

The SUV parked off to the side while the panel truck backed up to a side bay door. Neither had plates. Two men got out of the truck. Through her binoculars, she noted it was her friends from the gala. Then a third emerged from the SUV, and Jessie's stomach flipped.

Hastings.

He wore a black trench coat, collar up, hands in his pockets. Same smug gait. Same dead-cold stare that used to haunt her dreams back when she was under his command as he scanned the dock and the surrounding grounds.

"Son of a bitch," she muttered.

The others filed ahead of him, and Hastings touched his ear and spoke.

Spence continued typing furiously, nodding that he knew it was Hastings. "He's on the phone. Let's see what I can do. Give me twenty seconds."

His concentration was razor sharp—jaw clenched, eyes locked on the screen. No hesitation. No wasted motion.

Her mouth went dry. It was ridiculous, how attractive that was. How dangerous.

Focus, Mendoza.

Hastings walked up to the warehouse doors. One of the minions keyed in a code, and the panel slid open, swallowing them whole.

"They're inside," Jessie muttered. "What the hell are they doing here?"

The device in Spence's lap pinged once. "I've got audio."

Jessie leaned in closer.

Static crackled, then a voice came through—distorted but clear enough to make out Hastings' words. "...drones loaded and in position. Brewer wants the first wave en route to Berlin by midnight. Real-time deployment. We're taking the test units now. We hit the summit at 0800 before the idiots have even had breakfast."

Jessie's breath caught.

Berlin. A summit.

She glanced at Spence, and the grim look on his face confirmed it—this was a supply run. A damn prelude to that something big hovering in her stomach.

Brewer was about to make his move.

"There's a diplomatic summit at the Waldorf Astoria," Spence said, reading from his screen. "Thirteen nations are represented."

She swore again as Spence shared a few more tidbits from the newspaper article he was reading. Those attending the summit were a diverse group, comprising diplomats, cybersecurity experts, and representatives from billionaire tech startups.

The two minions reappeared, moving with purpose as they lifted heavy crates from a wheeled cart into the back of the panel truck. Jessie could see the stenciled markings on the side—serial numbers, air vents, ports.

Drones. No question.

Hastings filed out behind them, a set of papers in

hand, still on his call. "You want in? This is your last chance. In less than seventy-two hours, we'll be global."

Jessie's blood turned cold.

Global.

Not just Berlin. Not just a test.

Deployment.

Mass scale.

"Spence," she whispered, "we're out of time."

The panel truck rumbled to life, red taillights flaring through the mist as the back doors slammed shut.

"We have to follow them," she said, already shifting in her seat to check her weapon and slide her seatbelt on.

Spence didn't budge. His eyes were locked on the warehouse, not the truck. Hastings was still standing on the dock, cutting a deal with whoever was on the phone while flipping through the papers. "If we lose eyes on Hastings, we may not get another shot."

Jessie clenched her fists. "If Brewer's about to launch something that could torch Berlin and half the diplomatic core, we can't just sit here."

"I'm not saying that. I'll call for backup."

Backup? They were off the grid, and the other swans were too far away. "We'll lose them if we wait."

The truck pulled out, headlights vanishing down the service road. Her heart pounded against her ribs like a war drum. Hastings retreated inside.

Flynn's voice echoed in her mind. *If I disappear, go off-grid.*

Was he even still alive?

She turned to Spence and placed a hand on his arm—

not hard, just enough to make him look at her. "The time to hide behind that screen is over."

His jaw worked, and she knew what was going on in that massive tech brain of his. The warehouse. The truck. A thousand unknowns spinning in his head. Finally, he nodded once. Tight. Resolute. He handed her the tablet. "I've tapped into their GPS. Let's move."

Silently, she let out a relieved sigh.

They followed the panel truck at a cautious distance, their headlights off, their tires humming over the wet asphalt. Trees pressed in on either side, thick, looming silhouettes in the moonlight. Jessie gripped the edge of her seat, tracking the taillights as they dipped around a bend.

Spence eased their car around the curve and slowed. "Where the hell—?"

Ahead, a narrow road jutted into the woods. No signage. No lights. No movement.

And no taillights. The panel truck was gone.

"Son of a bitch." Spence clicked back to the last ping on the GPS tracker. "They blacked it out."

"They knew you were tracking them?"

He shook his head. "Not possible."

They crept forward, inch by inch, but the road was empty. Spence checked the dash display, tapped a few commands into the thermal sensors. Nothing.

Jessie stared at the hollow stretch of pavement ahead. No truck. No sounds. Just cold, wet silence.

She cursed under her breath. "We're not the only ones playing spy games tonight."

Her hand found the grip of her sidearm. Her pulse thumped in her ears, every nerve on edge. Something was wrong.

Very wrong.

The enemy had disappeared like smoke, and Jessie had the sinking feeling they'd just walked into a trap.

A trap she'd expected all along.

FOURTEEN

Spence

SPENCE EASED the car off the shoulder, gravel crunching beneath the tires. There had been taillights—two red dots bouncing ahead of them—and then there was nothing.

No turnoff. No brake lights. No sign of the road ending.

Gone. Like vapor. The GPS signal with them.

He let the engine idle. The forest around them was thick, pressing in on all sides, limbs clawing toward the car like skeletal arms in silhouette. His fingers clenched the steering wheel as his brain ran through possibilities.

Jessie leaned forward, scanning the shadowed road ahead. "Where the hell did they go?"

Spence reached for the onboard sensor array and toggled thermal imaging. Nothing but the residual heat from the road. No tire tracks. No heat signature. No vehicle hiding behind the trees.

Ghosted.

Jessie broke the silence. "This doesn't feel right."

Spence grunted. "It's a smart move, but I've seen better."

Her tone sharpened. "No, I mean this feels like a setup."

He stopped fiddling with the equipment. "You think Hastings knows we were watching?"

She didn't answer.

"You know him," Spence pressed. "Better than almost anyone. Could he have spotted our stakeout and led us here to pull us in?"

Jessie sat back in the seat, eyes still on the road like she was watching her own thoughts. "It's exactly the kind of misdirection Brewer pulled with my faked death, and when he wanted to get to Tessa. Throw up a flare in one direction, strike somewhere else. He must know all about me and Hastings. What if he's been using him to distract me?"

What he'd feared since the moment the truck disappeared. This was a psychological op. Brewer was gaming them. Yet, it didn't feel like a trap. Only, like she said, a distraction.

Spence exhaled slowly, reworking his strategy. "Then we don't get to make any more mistakes."

Jessie was quiet for a long moment. "You're right that we need to slow down and work this through. Maybe we should have stayed at the warehouse." She dug out her phone. "I'll call Langley and notify... Well, someone. We need to warn them about the impending attack."

He touched her hand, stopping her. "We don't know who to trust now, and we don't want to hand them an invite to the party just yet. If they act and scare off Brewer or Hastings, we lose them both."

"What about contacting someone in charge of the summit? They can call it off."

His hand was still on hers. He didn't move it. "We don't have any proof, only hearsay. They might not believe it, especially if word has already spread about Flynn's disappearance. We're part of a group that most of the world knows nothing about. Our word means zilch right now. But call Tessa. Tell her what we know and what we think. She has contacts in high places who can reach out to those attending the summit and give them a heads-up. What they decide to do with the info is up to them."

She grasped his hand, squeezing it. "You're good at this."

The compliment shot right to his gut. He returned the squeeze. "So are you, Agent Mendoza. I'm glad you're my partner."

They locked eyes. In the dim light, he saw her smile. Not a cocky smile, or a confident one. This was one he'd never seen before—a shy smile. She chuckled. It was breathy and sexy as hell. "I bet you say that to all the girls."

"For the record, I've never said that to anyone."

A pregnant silence fell. Her eyes dropped to his lips

again. She leaned forward. "Well, I'm glad you're my partner, too, Spence."

Like a magnet drawn to steel, he found himself moving toward her. His wildest fantasy—not about being on an op with her, but the one about kissing her—flashed through his mind. The moment was here. *Right now.*

But they were partners on a mission. He was technically her boss. And they were deep in the shit of an op that was likely to blow up in their faces if he didn't stop mooning over her and get his head on straight.

As if she sensed the myriad of reasons rolling on his internal screen like code, she did the one thing he didn't expect—she reached up with her other hand, grabbed him by the back of the head, and pulled him toward her.

The distance closed so quickly, he didn't have time to blink. One second, he was lost in her eyes, the next, her lips were on his.

They were soft—even warmer than he'd imagined. She tasted like heat and defiance, and the last sliver of sanity he hadn't already lost to her went out the proverbial window.

He didn't move at first. Didn't breathe. He was still computing, somewhere between logic and electricity, every nerve misfiring in disbelief. Then his hands slid into motion—one cupping her jaw, the other bracing against the console between them as he deepened the kiss with a low, hungry groan.

God, this wasn't supposed to happen. Not now. Not here. Not...

The second her fingers fisted in the front of his shirt,

he was gone. This wasn't fantasy anymore. It was real. *Too real*.

Everything he'd wanted for so damn long.

He kissed her like he'd been dying of thirst and she was the only clean water left on Earth. Like he didn't care what Brewer was planning or what awaited them down that road. There was only this. Her. Now.

Then—outside the car, a sudden screech.

Sharp and close, the sound cut through the moment like a blade. Both of them jolted.

Jessie pulled back, eyes wide. "What the hell was that?"

It took a moment for his brain to catch up. He knew that sound. "Screech owl," he said, breath ragged. "Nature's middle finger."

She blinked. Her hand was still on his chest. He was still at her jaw. Neither moved.

Then, as if the enormity of the situation hit them at once—the mission, the road, the missing truck—they both chuckled. An embarrassed, *what the hell did we just do* laugh.

Each turned away fast, staring out their respective windows like guilty teenagers caught making out in their parents' car. Spence scrubbed a hand over his face and blew out a shaky breath. "We've got to refocus."

"Yeah," Jessie said a tad too quickly.

He shifted in his seat and gestured between them. "Switch with me."

"What?"

"I need to get eyes on the map, start running local

scans. Time to see what's in this area, big enough to hide a panel truck. You drive."

She blinked. "You're trusting me with the wheel?"

"I just trusted you with my mouth. Don't make me rethink it."

She snorted and unbuckled, and they exited the car, the cool night air welcome on his overheated skin. As she passed him at the front of the vehicle, she brushed his hand, that shy smile playing on her face again.

As she settled into the driver's seat, Spence adjusted the passenger seat to fit his longer legs before he popped open the laptop, jaw still tight, mind split between the search for Brewer's next move and the lingering burn of her kiss.

Damn. If not for that screech owl's poor timing, he might still be lost in it.

Spence stared at the lines of code blinking across his screen, but his mind wasn't on the information. Not really. His fingers moved with muscle memory as he pinged surveillance grids and checked maps for local hiding places, but underneath it all, a storm brewed—dark, unrelenting.

The drones in that truck had been built with his AI blueprint. He'd built the architecture. He knew precisely how adaptable, how lethal it could be in the wrong hands. How had Harris Brewer gotten hold of it?

If this turned into an attack—if cities burned or people died—that blood would trail back to him. Not Langley. Not Black Swan.

Me.

He shoved the thought away. Images of Victoria flickered unbidden—five years old, clutching a ratty stuffed rabbit. Big eyes. Braver than she should've been. She was still out there. Somewhere. At least, that's what he told himself. That she was alive and well. If she ended up hurt because of this...

And dammit, he couldn't shake the gut-deep fear that he was failing Jessie at the same time—letting her walk into danger, thinking he could protect her.

"Where am I going?" she asked.

He snapped out of his spiraling thoughts. "Double back. Let me see if I can use the thermal to pick up any heat signatures."

A vehicle whizzed past.

"Wait," Jessie said, sitting up straighter. "That's the same SUV Hastings was driving."

Spence lifted his head and tried to catch sight of it, but the vehicle was moving too fast, headlights off, blending into the night like a phantom. What he did confirm? No license plate.

The tires bit into the road as Jessie whipped the car around and hit the gas. "It's him."

His body snapped back in the seat. "What are you doing?"

She gripped the wheel and leaned forward, squinting. "He'll lead us to the truck. Or Brewer."

"Jessie—" Spence shot her a glance. "You need to slow down. He could be leading us into a trap."

She kept her eyes locked ahead. "Then let him. I'm done wasting time."

His mouth opened to argue, but then he realized she wasn't a loose cannon. Not something he should—or could—rein in.

She was a guided missile.

And she might be the only one who could hit the target.

Securing his seatbelt, he turned back to his laptop and started tracking their course.

They followed the SUV for nearly twenty minutes, weaving out of the trees and into the fringes of the city. The roads widened. Streetlights flickered through the mist. Industrial buildings loomed—cold, silent monoliths in steel and concrete.

The SUV didn't speed or swerve. No evasive maneuvers. Hastings wasn't in a hurry, but he did seem to be on a schedule.

Maybe this wasn't a trap. Or perhaps Hastings was laughing all the way there, knowing he was drawing them deeper into it.

The SUV drove into a guarded site with a high chain-link fence topped with coils of razor wire. Beyond it stood a sleek, glass-and-metal structure that looked like it belonged in Silicon Valley, not the outskirts of Görlitz.

The name gleamed in silver against matte black glass. *Datenzentrum Nord.* Datacenter North.

Spence's eyes narrowed. "This is a private data facility. Top-tier. No government contracts, no outside access, full-scale biometric security. I didn't even know they had a node here."

Jessie parked in the shadows of a loading bay across the street. "What would Brewer want with a data vault?"

Spence's brain started spinning through possibilities. "If he's transferring the prototype, this is where he'd do it. Air-gapped systems. He could upload it to a cold server, then distribute it across a dozen dark net nodes."

"Or launch it from here?"

Spence nodded. "A logic bomb. A virus. Something designed to activate on a timer."

He scanned the building again, looking for the panel truck—but it wasn't there. Not parked. Not in the loading zone. "What if Hastings is freelancing?"

Jessie turned toward him, understanding dawning. "It would follow his MO—going out on his own and blackmailing his employer. You think he's double-crossing Brewer."

"It wouldn't be the first time he's burned someone, right? If this facility wasn't part of Brewer's plan, and Hastings is making a play, he could be selling the tech behind Brewer's back. This might be his headquarters. Or he may be hedging his bets, holding back evidence to blackmail Brewer or turn against him if needed down the road. Every law enforcement agency in the world wants Brewer in prison. If Hastings gets in a bind, flipping on Brewer could give him a Get Out of Jail Free card."

Spence reached for the laptop again, fingers flying. But the signal here was tight. Firewalled. He couldn't breach it from the car—not without drawing attention.

Jessie leaned forward. "So we sit and wait?"

Spence frowned.

"No," she said before he could respond. Her jaw set. "We go in."

He gaped at her. "We most certainly will not."

"We need to know what they're doing in there. Before sunrise. Before Berlin."

Spence stared through the windshield, tension coiling like wire in his gut. "The first thing you're going to do is call Tessa like we discussed."

"And what are you going to do? Play with your tech for the next hour because you're afraid to act like a field agent and actually shut this down now?"

The barb dug deep. He'd thought they'd made progress, but here they were again. She was ready to charge into a situation without knowing what that situation even was.

"I'm going to do what a good leader does—come up with a plan to breach the databank." He handed her her burner phone, smacking it into her palm when she accepted it. "And you're either going to cooperate and do this my way, or you're going to end up zip-tied and in the trunk. I'll breach alone. Your call, Agent Medoza."

FIFTEEN

Jessie

JESSIE'S FINGERS curled into her palms until her nails bit flesh.

Zip-tied and in the trunk?

He'd said it without blinking, voice cold enough to frost the windows. Not in jest, not as some flirty jab—he'd meant it. She'd seen the steel in his eyes, heard it in his voice.

The kiss was far away now. The connection they'd shared had snapped.

Her pride flared, hot and ugly, and underneath it came something heavier. Something she didn't want to name. A burr inside her chest, pricking and ripping at her heart. She tried to laugh, to brush it off, but the sound died in her throat.

He thought she was a liability. *Maybe he's right.*

Because as much as she wanted to tell herself she was still the same operative who'd bled and fought and survived alongside the rest of the swans, she wasn't.

She couldn't go back to being that agent ever again.

Not after Mosai Hagar's death squad had dragged her across concrete floors. Not after Brewer had leaned in close and told her in detail precisely what he would do to Tommy if she didn't do what he wanted. Not after she'd swallowed every ounce of fear she'd had and played the traitor to protect her brother.

That kind of betrayal—being used as a weapon against the people you'd die to protect—it didn't simply scrape at the surface of who you thought you were. It gutted you and left your morals and ethics on the ground to be stomped on.

And now?

She couldn't take orders without questioning the motive behind them. Couldn't follow a leader without calculating the odds of them stabbing her in the back. Couldn't be the swan she'd once been.

Maybe Spence saw that. Maybe since she'd returned, he'd *always* seen it.

Her pulse thumped hard. She gripped the door handle, not to get out, but to keep from doing something stupid—like slapping him just to make the hurt stop.

She turned to him, the glow from his laptop cutting sharp lines across his face. As always, he was calm and controlled. Already running ten mental scenarios while she was still chewing on the fact that he'd threatened to restrain her.

"Your way," she said, the words tasting like ashes on her tongue, "is to sit in the car and play with satellites while the bastards we're hunting waltz out with the keys to the apocalypse."

His hands stayed loose on the laptop, but his gaze was direct when it slid to hers. "My way is to keep us alive long enough to stop them. You want to rush in blind, go ahead—but you'll do it without me, and without the cover you'll need to get out."

That was the thing about Spence—he didn't raise his voice. He didn't have to. Every syllable smacked into her like a suppressed round.

She should've backed down. Should've played along until she could talk him into moving. That was the smart move.

Instead, her jaw locked. "I've been in tighter spots with less intel and walked out just fine."

"Not with Brewer on the other side of the door," he said. "He knows you. Knows your instincts. He and Hastings are counting on you to be predictable."

Dammit. She hated that he was right. Hated it so much she wanted to break something.

She also wanted to prove him wrong. *Needed* to prove him wrong.

How?

She leaned back in her seat, staring at the shadowed outline of the data center. Hastings inside. Was Brewer's code already worming its way into whatever servers they had hidden in there, or was it spidering out to locations all over the world? Every minute they waited was a minute he could be rewriting the rules of the game.

Spence wanted plans. Backup. Contingencies.

But what she saw—what she *felt*—was the narrowing window.

Brewer had already taken so much. Betraying his country and Tessa. Hurting her and threatening Tommy. Abusing and manipulating Jessie in order to turn her into a traitor...

More of his actions ticked off in her head: six months of the swans chasing him, along with multiple other agencies. Flynn, now missing. A summit in Berlin on the horizon, with a target painted on it the size of the Brandenburg Gate.

And if he succeeded—if those drones launched—it wouldn't matter how many contingencies they'd drawn up. In her mind, she saw a drone dropping a deadly virus on a crowd, a city skyline going dark, military installations being destroyed.

The fallout wouldn't be limited to Berlin or Munich. It would ripple through every city, every nation, every place she'd ever sworn to protect. Affect every person, from Tommy, whom she'd die to save, to the millions of people she'd never even met.

It wasn't impatience driving her. It was *necessity*. She had to act before the moment passed, before this chance was gone forever, altering her whole world. Didn't Spence understand that?

Brewer was a ghost. Hastings, too. If they were in

range, she had to take the shot. It might be the only one she ever got.

Her logical self—what was left of it—stepped in and handed her the justification on a silver platter. If she could get inside, even for a few minutes, she might get proof. Enough for Flynn. Enough to stop the summit. Enough to end this and nail Brewer to the wall.

And if Spence hated her for going off-script, she could live with that. Would live with it. He and the team could hate her all over again.

Her heart pinched. She shoved the hurt into the deep hole she'd dug for such things. There was no emotion that should stop her from doing the right thing.

Because the alternative was living with the deaths of millions of innocents on her conscience. Living with Tommy's, Tessa's, Meg and Dec's, and yes, even Spencer's.

No way in hell.

She would die to defend her country. To save Tommy and the others. All of the.

Die to protect Spence from ever going through what she had at the hands of manipulative bastards like Hastings and Brewer.

Because if they caught Spence, they'd force him to do unspeakable things. She knew firsthand just how they'd exploit his skills, use his weaknesses against him.

Spence turned the laptop and shifted toward her to show her the screen. "All right. Let's talk breach."

Jessie blinked, not expecting him to flip the switch so fast. "Breach?"

"It's just the two of us." He flicked his gaze to her before returning to the screen. "And yes, we're going in."

Her heart rate spiked at the fact that he was willing to take action, but she kept herself from getting too excited. She heard a 'but' coming in his tone.

"But we do it right." *Yep, there it is.* He pointed at the data center's internal layout, a blueprint, complete with ventilation runs, stairwells, and service corridors. "I hacked into the county building permits database. These are the schematics for the last structural upgrade they did."

She leaned in to scrutinize it. He smelled faintly of coffee and rain. And Spence. That tantalizing scent that was all his. It was steadiness mixed with adventure.

He slid the cursor to a spot on the west side of the building. "Security is tight. Lots of cameras, but not that many human guards. There's a service entrance here, with only two of them—one at the door, one on roving patrol. This hallway is our entry corridor. We avoid the main lobby—there's no employee on duty at this time of night, but there's a guard plus full camera coverage."

The cursor slid again, this time to an area that showed a narrow hallway cutting deep into the above-ground structure. There was a whole floor underground, too. "Hastings will most likely be somewhere in this block. That's where the offices are. If he's not there, he's below deck." He pointed to the underground level. "Here we have multiple hub partitions—he could be in any of them."

Every tidbit went into her mental copy of the blueprint, along with other things that might help her own plan if and when she had a chance to execute it. "Do we split up, then? I take the offices and you take the hub?"

"We do what we each do best. Once we're inside, I take control of the security cameras to keep them off you while you hunt for the proof we need. Photos. Audio, if possible. You know the drill. Once we have our proof, we extract here." He pointed to a loading bay on the opposite side of the building. "We slip out into the side street and use the tree line for cover. Ten minutes inside, max. No cowboy shit."

His eyes held hers when he said it, and for once, she didn't argue. She even nodded. It was a good plan. A safe one. Relatively safe. Things could go wrong. Probably would. If they did, she and Spence would have to improvise. "Sounds solid. What's our contingency if we get caught?"

"I create a distraction by setting off the fire alarms and coolant systems. If I can hack into their security system, I can also manipulate which areas get locked down, trapping the guards in certain locations. Resorting to violence is our last resort, but we go in locked and loaded in case these other options fail."

Damn. He was good at this job. She'd always known it, but it kept hitting her smack in the face. This plan was solid and could definitely work, but...

What if it didn't? What if they both ended up trapped inside with Hastings? What if they were both killed?

The best option was for one to go in and the other to

stay out here. "While this plan is solid and strategic, I have a suggestion."

He quirked a brow. "Of course you do."

"Hey, you're the one who keeps insisting we're partners. Do you want to hear it or not?"

He sat back and sighed. Motioned in a circle with his finger. "We are partners, and I welcome your input. Go ahead."

"Since there are only two of us, and our backup is still several hours away, you and I have to be a complete team. If the other swans were here, you'd stay put and keep an eye on things via your computer. The rest of us would complete the breach, and if things went belly up, you'd be our rescue."

He went still. "You want to go in alone."

She nodded, hoping against hope he would see the logic in it. She was making a valid point, even if the real reason was to initiate her own plan. "If I get caught, you're safe out here, and you can get me out. It makes more sense because we both know what the odds are of getting in and getting out unseen. If you put a cam on me, and I can get any sort of proof, though, before I get caught, you'll be able to share it with the world. "

His jaw ticked. He stared at the screen. For half a second, she thought he was actually considering it. "You and Hastings have too much history together. Plus, he might be screwing Brewer, and this is part of his plan. Or it could be a trap because he's realized you were at the gala tailing him. Too many variables. I can't in good conscience send you alone. Yes, I can manipulate a lot from out here. Still, with their security system, I need to get inside and plug into it to take control of cameras and allow you to move around without it setting off alarms and alerting the guards."

Damn. That put a crimp in her plan.

Still...

She'd faced worse odds before when breaking into a building, and she wasn't without her own hacking skills, even though they paled in comparison to his.

She pulled out her phone and called up Tessa's encrypted number.

Spence's gaze sharpened, but she typed and let him see the screen. *Possible breach. Outskirts of Görlitz, Data Center North. Meet us there as soon as you can.* She slid the phone back into her pocket. "Okay, that's done. Now, give me two minutes. I need to pee before we go play Ocean's Two."

He rolled his eyes and looked back at his computer. "Fine. I'll load a USB with a virus so we can play dirty and take the servers offline."

Again, he was so damn smart. She wouldn't have thought of that. Was she being an idiot to betray him?

The thought made her hesitate. He would never forgive her for what she was about to do.

The thought of those drones, though. Of Hastings and Brewer wrecking the world. Of innocent people being hurt or killed.

She checked her weapon. "Pop the trunk so I can grab another clip."

His eyes swung to her, and he hesitated. Her pulse

skipped. Was he reading her mind? Did he suspect what she was about to do?

But then he just gave a curt nod and hit the lever, releasing the trunk lid, before he returned to his typing.

She flung open the door before she lost her courage or let Spence's well-thought-out plan change her mind. Her boots hit wet gravel. While in the trunk's supplies of weapons, she did grab an extra clip for her handgun, along with the collapsible rifle, and a few clips for it, as well. Stashing it under her long coat, she closed the trunk and raced for the nearby trees.

The night air was suffocating, thick with humidity and the lingering rain. The line of conifers and pines was dense and dark, a perfect cover. If she cut the angle right, she could be inside before Spence even realized she'd gone off-script.

Because Spence's plan might be solid.

But hers?

Her plan was already air-tight.

SIXTEEN

Spence

THE MOMENT JESSIE slid out of the car, he knew.

It wasn't the "I have to pee" line—though that had been a nice touch—it was the way her body language had shifted half a second before she said it.

He'd played along and kept scrolling through the camera feeds, buying himself a moment before confirming what he already knew.

She was making a play without him.

His first instinct was the obvious one—call her out, order her to stand down, drag her into the trunk if he had to, like he'd threatened. But the second thought was stronger. *This is who she is now.*

Jessie was not the same swan who would run a plan into the ground before breaking ranks. Not the same partner who would back your play even when she hated it.

Brewer and Hagar had carved out pieces of her and replaced them with hard edges. He'd seen it in her eyes since they'd rescued her from Brewer—the calculation, the constant weighing of odds. And now here she was, betting it all on herself.

He leaned back in the seat, staring at the empty road.

Meg would read me the riot act.

Declan would tell me not to indulge her.

Flynn... Flynn would pull her off the op without hesitation.

But none of them were here. Just him.

He'd been where she was—hell-bent on a course no one could talk him out of. And when someone had tried, it had almost cost him everything.

In one area of his life, he continued to do it. Victoria. He would never stop searching for her, never stop hunting down the man who'd taken her.

Seconds ticked by. An eternity. Nearly as fast as his code could run a program, he ran through his options. His own personal code of morals and responsibilities.

Then he made the call.

He wasn't going to pull her back. He wasn't going to blow her cover by storming in after her.

He was going to make damn sure she got through that door without catching a bullet to the head.

Spence's fingers flew over the keys, the laptop already patched into the exterior feeds. The building's security network was airtight inside, but the perimeter? That he could touch.

He pulled up the live stream from the west side service entrance. The camera swept in slow, mechanical arcs, overlapping its field of vision with the one mounted at the corner of the loading dock.

Jessie wasn't in the frame yet. Good. If he could see her, someone else could, too.

He dove into the control menu and slid the feed into maintenance mode. The camera froze for a second—then resumed, but with a five-second loop of empty asphalt instead of real time. It would buy her the window she needed

She thought she was doing this solo. *Fat chance.*

He would always have her back. The decision was made right then and there. Even she went against his orders. Even if she went rogue.

He was all in.

He toggled to his secondary screen and powered up the thermal imaging scanner lying on the dash. A wash of heat signatures bled across the monitor in molten oranges and reds.

His pulse spiked. There—cutting low along the tree line, body heat muted by the damp night air. She was fast, fluid, and deliberate. Not reckless in her movements.

He tracked her until she dropped out of range, swallowed by the facility's blind spot. That was the last time he'd see her until she was inside. By then, if she screwed up, it would be too late to pull her out clean.

Spence swore under his breath, grabbed the thermal

gun, and sprinted to the trunk. There, he grabbed a Kevlar vest and loaded it with extra mags, a sidearm, and a knife.

Because if Jessie walked into hell, he was damn well walking in after her.

He slipped the vest over his head, the heavy weight distributing itself across his shoulders. Every mag, every weapon in the pouches, was a reminder of exactly how sideways this could go.

The logical move was to stay in the car, keep eyes on her through thermal, and be her safety net from a distance, just like she'd suggested. That's what Meg might do if she'd okay'd this, what Declan would demand if it had been his idea. Hell, it's what Flynn would have ordered if he were still around to give orders.

But again, this wasn't their call. *It's mine.*

And Jessie—bloody Jessie—was already inside, rushing toward a target who'd gutted her life once and still had the proverbial knife in his hand.

Spence racked the slide on his Glock, holstered it, and grabbed a suppressed SMG. A rifle would be better for long distance, but if they ended up in the server rooms, he'd need something compact.

He checked the thermal one last time—no sign of her now. She'd cleared the perimeter.

His gut twisted. This was where good leaders trusted their people. He slammed the trunk shut and stalked into the shadows.

The treeline swallowed him whole, the damp earth muffling his boots as he moved. He kept low, letting the black of his vest and jacket blend with the tree trunks. Even in the near-silence, his senses went razor-sharp—the faint hum of the facility's backup generators, the metallic tang of rain on steel, the distant hiss of tires on wet asphalt from the main road.

He skirted the arc of the parking lot lights, using the natural slope of the land to stay invisible. Ahead, the west side service entrance glowed faintly under a single halogen bulb, just enough illumination to silhouette anyone standing there.

Jessie was nowhere in sight. That meant she'd gotten past the guard post, and he didn't have to watch her try to improvise with a bullet in the mix.

He cut toward a cluster of utility sheds at the edge of the property. Maintenance outbuildings, they were likely filled with electrical panels, spare equipment, and maybe a way into the building that didn't require walking through a security checkpoint.

Every step, his mind ran through contingencies. The breach points, fallback routes, and how long it would take before his looped camera feed was noticed.

The west wall loomed closer. Spence pressed himself into the narrow strip of shadow beneath it, one hand on his Glock, the other fishing out a micro-drone from his vest. The object was the size of a matchbox, but its live feed might allow him to track Jessie without triggering the internal sensors.

He launched it low, letting it skim just above the grass. The tiny motor was a whisper under the rain.

The service door's keypad was a sterile blue rectangle

in the dark. A few feeet away lay an unconscious guard. Jessie's work, no doubt.

Spence crouched low, rain dripping from the edge of his hood, and slid a thin bypass tool from his pocket.

Four seconds to pop the cover. Another three to clip into the wiring. His laptop, slung across his chest on its strap, was already running a brute-force overlay. Numbers cycled in rapid succession on the screen.

Click.

The light shifted from blue to green.

Spence eased the door open an inch and stopped.

No movement. No sound but the hum of a vending machine somewhere down the hall and the distant vibration of HVAC units pumping climate-controlled air through the building.

He slipped inside, tugging the door shut behind him, and immediately hugged the wall. His eyes adjusted to the gloom—fluorescent strips buzzing overhead, their light patchy from bulbs that hadn't been changed in years.

The micro-drone's feed popped into the lower corner of his laptop screen. Grainy thermal imaging painted the interior in shades of white and gray. It caught a heat signature. Jessie's moving in a slow, calculated pattern. She was avoiding open spaces, keeping to the walls, checking corners before crossing. She was headed to the row of offices.

He moved in the opposite direction toward the doors to the basement server hub. If Hastings was here for data, that's where he'd be.

Stopping at one of the unattended guard stations, he stuck a USB into its computer. A special little code on it would have the place under Spence's control shortly, from the security cams to the fire alarms and suppressants.

Leaving it to do its job, he conducted another camera sweep on his scanner, froze the feed, and looped it just as before, buying himself a few more minutes before security noticed the blind spots. If they were even paying attention.

Somewhere ahead, a door clicked shut, the sound echoing down the corridor.

Spence's jaw tightened. That hadn't been Jessie.

Hastings? Possibly. Or a guard.

Either way, it was time to find out what exactly this data center had to do with Brewer's plan for the drones.

Jessie's thermal outline on Spence's scanner paused, then shifted toward a branching corridor—the same one his map said would loop her within thirty feet of the west stairwell.

And just beyond that stairwell...another heat signature.

Taller. Broader. Moving at a measured pace like a man who owned the place.

Hastings. Had to be.

Spence's gut knotted. If she kept going, she'd cross his path in under a minute.

They weren't wearing comms, so there was no way for him to alert her outside of intercepting her. The temptation to call her off was strong, but another part of him—

the one that had been doing this far too long—wanted to see what Hastings would do if he stumbled across her. How he'd play it. Whether she'd take him down or end up dead herself.

Of course, he wouldn't let that happen.

His ability to step back and see a bigger picture on missions—to look at them like a game on his computer—allowed him to stay unemotional even in the tightest and most dangerous situations. That made him an asset to the swans as much as his tech skills. Thanks to growing up under Ian Bastion's thumb, he'd learned early on to detach from any outcome because he could pretend it was a game.

Not with Jessie.

He eased forward, his boots making no sound on the polished concrete. The feed zoomed tighter on Hastings' heat signature as the two shapes drew closer. Jessie paused at the corridor's mouth, no doubt scanning for cameras or guards. She didn't know Spence was watching her every move, his pulse hammering in his ears.

Thirty feet.

Twenty.

Spence's finger twitched above the keys. He could use the building's internal comm system to warn her. Call her off or let it run?

The choice burned in his chest like acid. She could end up in Hastings' hands, or they might get the kind of proof they'd been chasing for months.

Jessie stepped forward, crossing the invisible threshold.

His fingers dropped to the keyboard. Just as he was about to force the fire alarms to go off, she stopped, backtracked.

He let out a breath.

The taller figure passed within a few feet of her. Jessie went on the move again, trailing him. If she played it right, she'd stay in the shadows.

Spence followed, only a few yards behind her. They cut through a maze of narrow hallways, past more closed doors.

The air grew cooler, tinged with the metallic bite of recycled ventilation. Somewhere below, a deep thrumming pulsed like a heartbeat—the unmistakable sound of high-density servers running at full throttle.

From the end of a long corridor, Spence watched as Hastings swiped a keycard at a reinforced steel door. A red light blinked to green, and the lock disengaged with a heavy thunk.

Jessie slipped out of a shadowed hall between him and where Hastings had entered and raced down to use a keycard on the lock. No doubt stolen from the downed guard outside.

She never looked back, or she would have spotted Spence. His long legs ate up the space, and he caught the door on the barest edge of it closing and eased it open enough to slide in.

A stairwell yawned before him, spiraling down into blue-lit gloom. The noise of the machines swelled, and voices—faint, quick, energized—echoed up from below.

Spence descended one step at a time, keeping to the

inside edge to minimize noise. From this vantage, he had both of them in sight: Jessie hugging the far wall, Hastings striding straight into an open den.

More voices and the smell of...pizza? Spence's hand went to his sidearm. Whatever waited in that basement, it wasn't just hardware.

SEVENTEEN

Jessie

JESSIE EASED down the narrow stairwell, keeping her weight on the edges of each step to kill the sound. The concrete was cool under her gloved fingertips, the air growing chillier with every foot she descended.

At the bottom, the space opened into a long, low-ceilinged room. Rows of black server racks stretched into the distance like sentinels, their blinking green and amber lights casting an otherworldly pulse. The air thrummed with the low, constant vibration of hundreds of processors working in unison.

She slid along the wall, her back brushing chilled metal piping. Somewhere ahead, the muffled clack of rapid keystrokes and quiet voices blended with the rhythmic hum of the cooling fans. The noise wasn't loud, but it was enough to mask her breathing and the whisper of her boots on the smooth floor.

Someone had ordered pepperoni pizza. The smell made her stomach growl. It turned sour when she spotted her target. Hastings' silhouette was instantly recognizable even in the dim light. Shoulders squared, gait confident, he moved between the server banks without hesitation. Never a glance over his shoulder. He knew exactly where he was going, and Jessie followed at the outer edge of the shadows, each step syncing with his.

She kept her weapon low, her grip steady. This wasn't just a server room—it was a vault. Whatever was happening down here wasn't meant to see daylight.

By now, Spence had to know she'd ditched him and the plan. She pictured him back in the car, jaw tight, eyes cold—either cursing her under his breath or already suiting up to come in after her.

She couldn't decide which would be worse.

If he stayed outside, he might contain the fallout. Keep them from getting burned. If he came in, they'd be two targets in a building full of unknowns.

But if she knew anything about Spencer Stirling, it was that he hated being left in the dark. And when it came to protecting the mission—and her—he wasn't the type to sit this one out.

She closed the gap by a few paces, close enough now to hear individual words in the murmured conversation up ahead.

If he came in after her, it would be for one of two

reasons—either to make sure she didn't screw this up, or to haul her ass out when things went sideways.

She wasn't sure which she hated more.

Because if it was the first, it meant he didn't trust her.

And if it was the second... it meant he cared enough to take the risk.

Neither sat comfortably in her chest.

Hastings rounded the last row of server racks and stepped into an open area at the far end of the basement. Jessie ghosted up to the corner and angled herself just enough to see without exposing her position.

A cluster of mismatched desks sat under industrial lights, wires snaking across the concrete floor like trip hazards. Five kids—no, young men and women barely in their twenties—were hunched over glowing monitors, each station a Frankenstein mashup of high-end rigs and assorted parts. Empty soda cans, energy drink bottles, half-eaten pizza slices, and bags of chips littered the surfaces.

The air was thicker here, warmer, the constant whir of fans joined by the rapid-fire clatter of keyboards. Monitors flashed with scrolling code, maps, login screens, and security dashboards. One kid wore a gaming headset plastered with stickers; another had duct tape holding his chair arm in place.

Jessie's gaze snapped to headset's screen where a bold header in English read: FEDERAL BUREAU OF INVESTIGATION – INTERNAL ACCESS PORTAL.

"I'm in," he yelled, grinning like he'd just won the lottery. "Full admin privileges."

The others broke into cheers and fist bumps.

"What do you want me to do, boss?" the kid asked Hastings. "Scrape every agent profile or wipe the Feds' whole database of terrorists?"

Jessie's pulse kicked hard. Wiping the Bureau's data could cripple hundreds of ongoing investigations. But scraping it? That would give them intel on every single agent—names, addresses, assignments.

Hastings barely glanced at the kid. "Do what you want with the Bureau." He leaned on the back of another chair, eyes on a different monitor. "But the first one of you to breach Langley's mainframe gets a ten-grand bonus."

Jessie froze, every muscle locking tight.

Brewer wanted global chaos.

Hastings wanted the CIA.

She gripped her Glock tighter. She could step out right now, plant one in Hastings's leg, and end this before his little hacker club burrowed into Langley.

Her breathing slowed, her training pressing down hard on the adrenaline urging her forward.

Five hackers. One Hastings. None of them looked dangerous in a physical sense—soft bodies, caffeine jitters, posture wrecked by too many hours at a desk—but there was nothing harmless about the firepower at their fingertips. A single keystroke could open back doors, wipe files, and expose every federal agent to the world.

And even if she stopped this party, she'd bet good

money that all of the hackers' codes and programs were stored on the cloud somewhere. If even one of them escaped—and the odds were high that several would—they could still carry out Hastings' plan.

She'd faced worse odds. Hell, she'd survived worse odds. But that had been before everything Brewer had done to her, before her trust in herself had been chipped down to splinters.

And then there was Spence.

He had to be somewhere in the building. Watching? Tracking her? She could almost hear him in her head—*don't rush in blind, J, make it a win, not a suicide run.*

She clenched her jaw.

This was Hastings, the man who'd taught her tradecraft before turning on everything they'd stood for. Every instinct screamed to take the shot, to finish it now. But instincts were exactly what Brewer and Hastings counted on.

Her gaze drifted back to the glowing screens, lines of code flickering faster than her eyes could follow. Langley was the big prize. If they got in, the fallout wouldn't just be career-ending for every agent in the field—it would be life-ending for some.

She couldn't risk being taken down here, in this basement, before warning Spence and the others. He'd have a plan for neutralizing the threat without handing them her corpse as a consolation prize. And as much as it burned her to admit it, his approach was often the best one.

She eased back into the shadows, muscles tight, forcing herself to retreat instead of engage.

For now.

Jessie shifted her weight, careful not to scuff her boot against the concrete. She took one step back. Then another.

From somewhere behind the row of server racks, Hastings's voice carried to her. "Where's the guard that should be outside the door?"

"Said it was break time," one of the women said. "Guess he's taking a long one."

Hastings grunted, but it had the edge of suspicion to it.

The guard she'd incapacitated. *Shit.*

She turned toward a bank of giant servers to slip through them and see if she would find another exit. Hastings would be too antsy about the one they'd both entered through, and keeping an eye on it. She needed a new way out.

A shadow detached itself from the gloom at the end.

Tall. Broad. Familiar.

Spence.

God, he was going to kill her, but she was both relieved and annoyed that he was here. In the basement. Watching her.

Their eyes locked across the dim glow of the spill-light. He gave the slightest shake of his head—*don't blow it*—and then he was gone again, melting back into the darkness as silently as he'd appeared.

Jessie's pulse kicked up. Where was he going? She

moved to follow, like a shadow between the racks of humming servers. She quickened her pace, rounded the end...

And froze at the cold press of steel against her temple.

"Evening, Agent Mendoza," Hastings murmured, voice oily with satisfaction. "What an interesting surprise."

She didn't move. Didn't breathe. The gun was as real as the hand on her arm steering her forward.

"I take it you're the reason my guard has disappeared. One of my tricks, I bet. You always were a good student." He disarmed her and pushed her ahead of him. "Let's not make a scene. Walk."

He guided her past the servers into the hackers' den. "Ladies and gentlemen," Hastings announced, "we have company." He shoved her into a chair, the metal legs screeching against the concrete. "Meet the legendary Jessie Mendoza—traitor, survivor, and, if the rumors are true, the only one Harris Brewer has failed to break completely."

The kids smirked, barely looking up from their keyboards. Hastings leaned against the table beside her, both guns in hand, casual as a cat with a cornered mouse.

"That's the trouble with legends," he said. "Eventually, you run out of luck."

"Now that's ironic, mate," a familiar voice said from off to her side. "I was just about to say the same thing about you."

Hastings stood and stiffened, his eyes cutting toward

the dark aisle of server racks. Around the table, computer alarms began going off, the hackers turning frantic eyes on their screens as they began pounding at the keyboards. "What the...?" one said. Another, "I'm locked out!"

Spence stepped into the light, holding up a slim flash drive, expression carved from stone. "I've just shut down your fire sale operation and given each and every one of your minions here a virus that will corrupt their codes and programs." He winked at Jessie. "Guess that bonus you were going to give one of them will have to go toward your attorney fees."

EIGHTEEN

Spence

HASTINGS' smirk didn't waver, but the way his fingers flexed on the pistol told Spence he was already recalculating.

"I heard you enjoy the dramatic entrance, Stirling," he drawled. "Tell me—did you practice that little speech in the mirror, or did it just come to you while you were babysitting your trigger-happy swan?"

Jessie stiffened at the jab. She didn't look at Spence, but he caught the subtle shift in her posture—shoulders loose, chin dipped, back straight and ready to pounce.

Spence ignored the bait and nodded toward the hackers, still hammering frantically at their keyboards as error messages multiplied across their screens. "Call them off, Hastings. Before I decide, this virus gets hungrier."

Hastings gave a lazy shrug. "You think I care about

them? They're replaceable. Always have been." His gaze slid to Jessie, hard and calculating. "She's the interesting one. Pretty, dangerous, and if I'm gauging that killer look in her eyes, still loyal enough to throw herself in front of you. I wonder what it would take to break that."

Spence's jaw locked. "Don't test me."

"Oh, I think I will." Hastings shifted his weight just enough to make every muscle in Spence's back coil tight. "Let's see how dirty you want to fight."

Spence took a slow step forward, angling himself so Hastings had to pivot to keep the gun lined up. "You know what you are, Hastings? You're a petty ex-Agency employee with a bruised ego. Brewer's playing on the world stage, and you're down here in the basement like some wannabe Bond villain, running side hustles and nursing your grudge against Langley."

Hastings' eyes narrowed, the muscle in his jaw twitching.

"You're not even in his league," Spence pressed. "Brewer wants to control the future. You?" He let the word hang like a bad smell. "You're just hoping the Agency notices you long enough to admit they were wrong about you. Spoiler alert—they weren't. You were never good enough for anything more than running a few noncritical missions. Hell, you weren't even good enough to work solo."

Hastings' smirk faltered, replaced by something harder, uglier.

"Does Brewer even know about this side gig?" Spence asked, tilting his head toward the hackers. "Or are you hoping you can sell the intel before he finds out? Guess we'll see who kills you first."

That did it. The flash of rage in Hastings' eyes came with a sharp, deliberate motion—he swung the gun away from Jessie and leveled both weapons square at Spence's chest. Walked toward him.

Just like Spence wanted.

Jessie moved like lightning. She kicked the leg of the chair next to her, sending it toppling with a crash. The noise ricocheted around the server room, pulling Hastings' aim just a fraction off-center.

Spence lunged.

The guns went off—loud, concussive, close enough to make his ears ring. The hackers shrieked, diving under their table.

Pain exploded through his right hand as his palm smacked against the barrel in mid-grapple, but he kept driving forward, momentum carrying both men into the edge of a server rack.

The server rack shuddered from the impact, plastic casing cracking as metal screamed. Spence's shoulder took the brunt. Hastings fought like a man possessed.

One gun clattered to the floor. Spence went for it, but Hastings slammed a forearm across his throat, driving him back against the rack.

Pain flared white-hot along his windpipe. He jerked his knee up, catching Hastings in the thigh, and shoved back hard enough to break the chokehold. Hastings retaliated with a wild right hook, and Spence ducked. The blow glanced off the side of his skull, but still rattled his teeth.

He swung with his right hand, aiming for Hastings' jaw. The connection was hard enough to ring his bell. The other gun dropped, but something popped in Spence's wrist. His fingers went numb, a sick heat radiating up into his forearm. Agony ripped from wrist to fingertip.

Hastings saw it.

He caught Spence's right hand in both of his and wrenched it back at an angle hands weren't meant to go. Bone grated—a sharp, tearing sensation shot through the tendons.

Spence's vision narrowed to a tunnel. He snarled through the pain, shifted his weight, and slammed his left fist into Hastings' ribs—once, twice—until the other man's grip loosened.

Jessie was shouting something—his name, maybe—but the roar of blood in his ears made it sound far away.

The guns were still on the floor; one had been kicked closer to Jessie during the scuffle. Hastings realized it at the same time Spence did.

Both men lunged.

Jessie beat them both. One hard kick sent the gun skittering under the hacker table. Hastings swore, lunging after it.

Spence used the opening. He hooked his left arm around Hastings' neck in a brutal half-clinch and drove him backward, slamming him into the edge of the server rack. The impact sent a ripple of blinking lights across the consoles.

Hackers ran for the door. Jessie grabbed and pointed her weapon, but couldn't get a clear shot.

Hastings twisted, elbowing Spence square in the ribs. Pain exploded in his side, but it was nothing compared to the raw fire chewing through his right hand every time it so much as twitched. Jessie tossed him her gun. Spence caught it with his left hand and brought it down on Hastings' skull.

The man staggered, grabbing his head. Blood oozed through his fingers. An alarm sounded—at least one of the guards had realized what was going on.

Jessie darted past them, grabbed the flash drive from where Spence had dropped it, and yanked him toward the far aisle. She snatched her gun from his hand. "We need to go!"

He couldn't let Hastings get by with this, but her grip was firm enough to keep him off balance. He staggered, adrenaline dulling the pain enough to keep his feet under him. "I've got to take care of..."

Hastings pushed off the rack and came after them, fury etched deep into every line of his face.

"Him," Spence finished.

Gunfire erupted—sharp, deafening in the narrow space. Bullets punched into the steel wall inches from Jessie's shoulder. She ducked, fired back.

Hastings went down.

Spence shoved her through the doorway and yanked it shut. "Go!"

They pounded down the corridor, past coolant pipes and stacked crates. A guard popped out and raised a weapon. Jessie nailed him center mass and lobbed a grenade back toward the server rooms.

Every throb of his right hand felt like a countdown clock ticking louder in his skull. The injury was severe. His wrist might be broken. And without it, hacking into anything at the speed they'd need would be like fighting with one eye shut.

But that was a problem for the next breath. For now, the only mission was simple—get him and Jessie out alive.

A corridor led to an exit on the side of the hill. They burst through it, the cool night air a welcome relief. Gravel crunched under their boots as they tore across the narrow service lot, past the gated entrance, and toward the car.

Inside, the grenade exploded, sending up a huge fireball.

Shouts erupted behind them, sharp German curses slicing the dark. Spence risked a glance back and saw two guards in tactical gear closing fast, rifles already coming up.

Jessie's hand clamped on his arm, shoving him toward the passenger side. "Come on!"

He wanted to argue, but his right hand was throbbing so hard it made his vision swim. The weapon slung over his shoulder banged against his ribs as he ducked into the seat.

She yanked his suppressed machine gun free before

he could get a grip on it. "Hope you've got the exit plan ready."

With a smooth, practiced motion, she stepped back from the car and opened fire in controlled bursts. The sharp cough of the suppressor was almost lost under the pounding of Spence's pulse. Muzzle flashes lit her face in strobes, showing her narrowed eyes, set mouth, and total lethal focus.

It was hard not to appreciate it.

The guards dove for cover, pinned behind a low wall as rounds from the gun chewed the concrete inches from their heads. Jessie didn't waste a second. She vaulted around to the driver's side, ducked into the seat, jammed the gearshift into reverse, and slammed her foot down.

The tires squealed, the car fishtailing before she threw it into first and shot forward.

Spence's head snapped toward her as she reached into her coat pocket. "Jess—"

She pulled the pin on a hand grenade with her teeth and lobbed it through the still-open driver's window toward the building's side entrance.

Damn, how many of the bloody things had she lifted from the trunk?

They were a hundred yards out when the world behind them turned white.

The explosion punched through the night, a rolling wave of fire and smoke blooming against the sky. The shockwave rattled the car, shards of glass and debris pinging off the roof as Jessie gunned it down the empty road.

In the rearview, the building vomited black smoke into the stars.

Spence slumped back against the seat. Jessie's knuckles were white on the wheel, her jaw clenched. "Which way?" she demanded.

"East for now." He closed his eyes for a brief moment. "Once we're sure we don't have a tail, we'll hit the safe house."

"Is he..." She shifted, and the car lurched. "Do you think Hastings is dead?"

Pivoting in the seat and ignoring his worthless wrist, he squinted back at the data center. Another explosion occurred when something struck a gas line. "I wouldn't bet money on it."

"And the drones? Will Brewer still launch them in the morning?"

Another unknown. But now, if Hastings *was* alive, they had a way to blackmail him with Brewer. "No one is safe until we deactivate them." It was the best he could do. He raised his injured hand. "And that's going to be a challenge for me, now."

Her gaze flicked to him. She grimaced. "You need a doctor."

They hit the highway and flew down the blacktop, the rain reflecting their headlights when Jessie flipped them on. "No hospitals," he said. "No doctors. We're off-grid, now, remember? Those places want information and answers I can't give."

But, holy mother, he needed some pain meds.

"This is all my fault," she said softly. "I should have stayed in the car."

He gritted his teeth so he didn't lip off, *You think?* Bloody hell. "We stopped them, at least for now, from breaching any other U.S. intelligence service."

"Did we? Won't they have backups of their programs?"

"The virus I left them with will wipe out their cloud, as well as anything directly tied into those servers." He grimaced as he shucked off his vest and tossed it in the backseat. "I'm sure Hastings' pets have off-site backups, but for now, they're out of commission until they can regroup."

She fell silent as he programmed in a new route into the GPS to take them on a circular path back to the apartment. It was awkward since he had to use his left hand.

When he sat back and she seemed assured no one was following, she said, "Go ahead."

He sank deeper into his seat, cradling his arm. "Go ahead, what?"

"Yell at me. I deserve it."

She did, too. And he was furious.

But he'd let her put him in that situation. He'd made the call, and this was the outcome.

Stupid.

Some leader he was.

"We'll discuss it later." He closed his eyes and clenched his jaw. "Right now, we need to regroup."

She started to say something, and he raised a hand to stop her. Silence fell; the only sounds were the tires on the wet road and the GPS telling them to turn right in half a kilometer.

Spence focused his anger on Hastings rather than Jessie. They had more intel now on him, and had delayed his attempts to break into the CIA, but was he the one who'd breached the Pentagon's security? Was he using Brewer's signature as his own?

Did Brewer know?

All questions had to wait. Until he could get back up to speed, they were lame ducks. He sneaked a peek at Jessie. By her expression, she knew it, too.

And was blaming herself.

For now, he planned to let her stew.

Which was either a tactical move...or a dangerous one.

NINETEEN

Jessie

THE APARTMENT WAS silent when they slipped inside. It should have been comforting, but the contrast made Jessie's skin itch. It was too quiet, too normal after the chaos they'd just left behind.

Her boots felt heavy on the warped wood floor. Her ankle was tweaking again, too. Spence's footsteps were quieter, but every movement was tight. He kept his injured wrist tucked close to his body, and there was a grim set to his mouth.

She shut the door and slid the bolt home, eyes still on him. He didn't look at her. Didn't say a damn word. Just crossed to the small table to set down his laptop and open it. The glow from the screen threw sharp lines across his face as he dropped into the chair.

The knot in her chest tightened.

It was worse than if he would yell. If he'd tear into her for ditching the plan, she could push back, fight him on it. But this? This cold, quiet distance? It was a wall, and she hated it.

Her fingers twitched at her sides. She wanted to fill the silence, but what would she say? *Sorry, I almost got you killed? Sorry, your wrist looks like a balloon because of me?*

Instead, she stood there, taking in the sight of him working one-handed, and awkwardly at that, jaw tight as he navigated the keyboard with his left. Every slow, methodical click of the keys sounded too loud in the cramped room.

Her guilt clawed higher.

"We need to wrap your wrist and get ice on it," she said finally, her voice rougher than she meant. "Your hand isn't going to fix itself."

He didn't look up. "It'll hold."

She stepped into his space and grabbed his left arm, tugging him to his feet. "Yeah, until you try to use it and it gets worse. Couch. Now."

That earned her a flick of his eyes, which were guarded and unreadable, before he pushed back from the desk with a sigh and stood.

She told herself it wasn't victory she felt. It was just relief that he'd listened.

She guided him to the couch, the springs squeaking under his weight. His jacket came off with a rough shrug, and she caught the faint hiss of pain he didn't quite swallow.

"Shirt off," she said.

One brow arched. "That's a bold opener, even for you."

She rolled her eyes, but heat crept up the back of her neck. "The cuff of your shirt is too tight to push up, and we need to remove it now before your wrist swells too much to get it off entirely. We'll find you something looser."

His smirk was faint, but it lingered as he peeled the long-sleeved black shirt over his head, needing her help to ease the cuff off of his swollen hand. It left him bare from the waist up. The sight punched the air right out of her lungs. Broad chest, lean muscle, the kind of strength that didn't come from a gym but from years of using his body as a weapon.

She made herself focus on the hand, all mottled with bruising, the wrist stiff and unyielding. "Hastings did a number on it," she murmured, crouching in front of him.

The small first aid kit was on the coffee table. She dug out an instant cold pack, smacking it until it went rigid with ice. Bending down in front of him, she pressed it gently to his wrist, where it rested on his knee.

His sharp inhale brushed the top of her head.

"Sorry," she said automatically.

"Don't be. Just...finish what you started."

It wasn't about the wrist anymore, not with the way his voice dropped, low and rough, curling around her spine.

Her pulse jumped. She adjusted the pack, gently wrapping it in an elastic bandage to hold it in place, her fingers brushing his skin with every pass. Warmth radiated from him, seeping into her palms, her chest.

When she glanced up, his gaze was locked on her. Not guarded anymore. Not even angry. Just...watching.

It was enough to make her fumble the bandage, her fingertips skating over the rugged ridge of muscle in his forearm before she caught herself.

She cleared her throat. "You need some pain meds?"

"There's nothing in the kit that's strong enough."

"There is if you wash them down with bourbon."

His mouth curved, slow and dangerous. "Are you trying to get me drunk so I don't yell at you? Or so you can take advantage of me?"

Gah. He was intolerable. And so was her traitor of a pulse. It had sped up to a ridiculous beat, and she couldn't seem to keep her eyes off his pecs, his abs. "You wish."

To get a better angle, she shifted to sit next to him. Her fingers faltered, suddenly hyper-aware of how close they were, how her knees brushed his thigh. She should've moved away. She didn't. *Focus.* "You're lucky you didn't break it completely," she said. "Or your fingers."

"Would've been worth it if I'd at least put Hastings down for good."

Her mouth tightened. "Or you could've avoided getting hurt in the first place if you'd just let me handle it my way."

His eyes sharpened, the warmth from a moment ago cooling fast. "Your way got you cornered in a room full of hackers and a man holding a gun to your head. I got you out alive."

"I was never *not* getting out alive," she snapped.

He leaned in, bracing his left hand on the couch beside her hip. "That's the problem. You think you're untouchable. That nobody can corner you, outthink you, or break you. Newsflash, Jessie—you're not."

Her breath came faster, anger and something darker twisting together. "You think I don't know that? You think I haven't lived it? I've been broken, Spence. I've been used. And the only reason I'm still here is because I stopped letting other people decide how I play the game."

They were nose to nose now, the air between them charged and tight.

He didn't back down. "You're here because the swans caught you and forced you out of the situation with Brewer. Otherwise, you might still be under his thumb."

That was technically true, but... "I had a plan to get away from him and protect Tommy, too. You guys just showed up before I got to enact it."

"Sure." His voice was dismissive. He didn't buy it. "Well, one of these days, you're going to push things too far and I won't be there to pull you out."

The words should've pissed her off more. Instead, they hit like a sucker punch, because buried in them was something she hadn't expected. *Fear.*

He was scared. For her.

Her voice dropped a notch. "And yet, you're still here."

His gaze zeroed in on her mouth. "Yeah," he said roughly. "I am."

She didn't remember who moved first—maybe it was both of them—but the distance vanished. His good hand slid to the back of her neck. Her fingers fisted in his short hair. And the kiss landed like a collision neither of them could stop.

His mouth was hot and demanding, tasting faintly of coffee and adrenaline. She met him with equal force, months of tension and unspoken need igniting all at once. His hand slid down her spine, fingers splaying at her lower back, pulling her closer until she was straddling his lap, her knees pressed into the couch cushions on either side of him.

The bandage on his wrist brushed her hip. He hissed —not from the pain, but from the way she ground against him.

Her pulse thundered. "Tell me this is a bad idea," she whispered against his lips.

His eyes burned into hers. "It's the worst idea I've ever had." His thumb traced the line of her jaw. "But hell if I'm stopping, luv. If this is what *you* truly want."

She kissed him again, deeper this time, letting go of the last of her defenses. He tasted like every dangerous thing she should've walked away from and didn't. Her hands roamed over his chest, mapping the hard planes there, soaking up the warmth of his skin.

He groaned, low and rough, and shifted them, pinning her beneath him. His weight came over her— solid, steady, protective. For once, she didn't resent it.

Her T-shirt was gone before she realized he'd even tugged it over her head, his mouth finding the sensitive spot just below her collarbone. She arched into him.

"You drive me mad," he murmured against her skin.

"Good," she breathed, her nails grazing his shoulders. "Just so you know, this is only the beginning."

His laugh was short, almost disbelieving, before he claimed her mouth again. Every kiss was a battle for control, and neither of them was willing to lose.

His injured wrist kept him from stripping off her pants and his, but he allowed her to do the honors. When they were both naked, it didn't stop him from touching her everywhere. And she let him, because in this moment, there was no Brewer, no Hastings, no summit in Berlin. Just them, and the fire they'd been holding back for far too long.

When he finally pushed inside her, it wasn't gentle. It was a surge, a claim, a promise that he was done pretending he didn't want this.

She met him thrust for thrust, her fingers clutching his back, her breath coming in broken gasps.

"J..." His voice cracked on that letter, that nickname, the sound enough to unravel her completely.

The rest was heat and motion, the kind of connection that burned through every wall they'd built. "Come for me," she demanded.

He did, taking her with him. The height of pleasure gave way to a deep dive into an abyss. It had been so long —too long—and she never wanted to come out of it again.

When it was over, she lay tangled in his arms, her

cheek on his shoulder, his heartbeat pounding as hard as hers. Neither of them spoke.

Jessie closed her eyes and ignored the voice nagging at her. Nothing between them would be the same after this.

She could only pray it would be better.

That she could be better.

She wanted to be the partner that Spence would be proud of.

TWENTY

Spence

THE APARTMENT WAS quiet except for the faint hum of distant cars carrying early commuters and the muted click of his left index finger on the trackpad. Jessie was curled on the couch across from him, one knee hooked over the blanket, hair mussed from sleep. She'd kicked the quilt half off somewhere between their love-making and now, leaving it tangled around her legs.

An hour ago, she'd been warm in his arms, her breathing ragged against his ear. Now she was still, chest rising and falling in slow rhythm, lashes resting on bruised cheekbones. She looked peaceful.

He wished he could make it last.

Shifting in the chair, the cushion springs creaked under his weight. His right wrist continued to ache, wrapped tight in bandages and tucked against his chest.

Hen-pecking with his left hand was slow, sloppy work, but he'd take that over sitting here doing nothing.

His screen was a mess of open tabs—encrypted news feeds, dark web boards, back-channel chatter. He was hunting for any hint about the Data Center North fire.

So far, nothing concrete. Local media were referring to it as an "industrial incident." One outlet mentioned "possible arson" but had no details. No mention of Hastings. No mention of a firefight.

Spence wasn't naïve enough to think that meant they were in the clear. Silence just meant whoever was cleaning it up was doing a damn good job.

Hastings? Brewer?

He glanced at Jessie again. She'd survived things most operatives wouldn't walk away from. Still, every instinct in him wanted to keep her like this—out of the line of fire, breathing easy.

Neither of them was built for easy.

Three knocks came at the door. A pause. Two more.

Spence's head jerked toward the entrance. His hand stilled on the keys.

Jessie stirred, muttering something in her sleep.

The knock came again—three, pause, two—sharper and more deliberate.

His pulse kicked. It was a code.

He'd sent instructions hours ago in a scrambled text to Tessa and Tommy, along with the facts of their situation. *Abandoned target. Safe house secure. Meet there.*

If they were here, it was faster than he'd expected.

Jessie's eyes cracked open, blinking against the dim light. "Spence—?"

He raised a finger to his lips and slid out of the chair without a sound. The hardwood floor creaked under his weight, so he hugged the wall, keeping his movements controlled.

His gun was in hand. The injury slowed some things, but not that. Any decent agent could shoot with either. The cold steel felt almost comforting in his palm as he moved toward the door.

The shadows in the hallway outside the peephole shifted.

Could be them. Could also be someone who'd been able to intercept the message. He unlatched the deadbolt, keeping the chain engaged. "Yeah?"

A low voice came back, calm, steady. "I brought the sugar you ordered."

Tessa's voice. He'd know that tone anywhere—dry, faintly amused, but with an edge that said she was ready for trouble.

He slid the chain free and opened the door. Tessa and Tommy slipped inside like they'd done it a thousand times. Both were dressed in dark jackets, cargo pants with full pockets, and boots scuffed from travel. Tommy carried a duffel that could easily have been stuffed with gear or explosives.

Jessie sat up, rubbing her eyes and yawning. "You made good time."

"Didn't exactly stop for sightseeing," Tessa said. "Now tell us what the hell happened."

Tessa didn't bother taking off her coat before she claimed the arm of the couch. Tommy dropped his duffel beside the coffee table and crouched to unzip it. Inside, Spence caught a glimpse of weapons, extra comms gear, and a portable jammer. Always prepared.

Jessie got up and hugged him. He gripped her back, hard. She yawned again and plopped down on the cushion, raising a bare foot to brace it on the table. "We tailed Hastings to a private data center. He had a crew of hackers in the basement—kids. One of them breached the FBI's internal database while I watched. But Hastings was after the CIA."

Tommy's head snapped up. "Langley?"

"That's what it looks like," Spence said. "I dropped a virus in their system. Wiped everything they had before they could do any harm. But it's possible Hastings got away. I can't confirm his death."

Tessa swore under her breath. "And Brewer?"

"No sign of him," Jessie said. "It appears that Hastings has his own agenda, and it may be tangled with Brewer's, but Brewer may not know anything about it, either."

Tessa made a face that showed she was mildly impressed.

The vibration in Spence's pocket got all of their attentions. He pulled out his phone with his good hand, saw the encrypted incoming call, and gave a sharp nod. "It's Dec."

He hit the speaker. "Go."

"We're in Munich," Declan's voice came, battle-worn and impatient over the static. "Location?"

Jessie shot Spence a questioning look, but he didn't hesitate. "Dropping you a pin now. ETA?"

A pause. "Five minutes."

Exactly four and a half minutes later, the knock came —different rhythm this time, quick and light. Spence opened up and ushered in Meg and Dec, cool, humid air following them.

Acknowledgments were made quickly. Meg pulled off her gloves as she crossed to the table. "As soon as we landed, I got an encrypted message. I think it was from Flynn."

Jessie straightened. "What did it say?"

"That the Brewer lookalike I saw in D.C. is the real deal."

Spence's gut tightened. "That can't be right. I'm sure he's here."

Jessie nodded in agreement. "If he's planning something for the summit, he'll want to be there to watch it happen. That's how he operates." She glanced at the cuckoo clock. "And we're running out of time to stop it."

That's when it hit Spence like a flashbulb.

"He's done it before," he said, almost to himself. "He throws up a flare in one place and hits the real target somewhere else."

"What are you talking about?" Dec grunted.

Jessie went rigid and snapped her fingers. "That's exactly it. Brewer wants us to believe he's here so he can get all of *us* here. Meanwhile, he's also managed to get rid of Flynn." She glanced at each of them in turn. "Hastings isn't the only one going after the CIA. *That's* Brewer's real target."

The room went silent.

"Shit," Tommy said under his breath.

Tessa scrubbed her hands through her hair. "That can't be right. He wants to take over the world."

"He has a grudge against the Agency that could sink the Titanic," Jessie countered. "Hastings, too. Together, they're a formidable pair. Deadly. If they get revenge on the CIA, think of what else they can do."

Dec paced and swore. "Brewer's good, you have to give it to him. He's completely fooled us, making us believe he's trying to take over the world, when the only thing he really wants is—"

"To destroy Langley," Meg finished for him.

Jessie leaned her elbows on her knees. "Not the only thing. He still wants to ruin the world and then come in like a savior to rescue it, but I'd bet money that taking down the CIA is the first step."

"And now, we're all here," Meg said, "when we need to be in Virginia."

Tessa rubbed her face with her hands. "That bastard. That goddamn bastard! How did he do it? How did he fool us yet again?"

Spence leaned forward, laying his bad wrist on his knee. "Because he didn't just feed us bad intel—he made us want to believe it. Berlin was always the loud target. Langley's been the quiet one. We took the bait."

Jessie crossed her arms, chin tucked low in thought.

"If he gets inside Langley, it's not just names and missions. It's black files, embedded assets, deep cover ops —everything. Every country we have a footprint in is compromised."

"And every operative in them, dead," Tessa added grimly.

Dec stopped pacing and turned toward Spence. "Then we can't waste another second. We need to figure out where and how he's going to hit Langley, and we need to do it before he even boots up his system."

Tommy nodded toward Spence's laptop. "What do you need?"

"Access," Spence said. "And time. Both of which are in short supply." He looked around the room. "I can get us on a plane back to the States in an hour, maybe two. It may not be soon enough, but it's all we can do."

Meg shook her head. "Too risky. We're probably on the no-fly lists. Dec and I came over on a private plane, thanks to a connection of mine, but there's no round-trip option."

"You forget that I had a life before I joined the CIA." Spence pecked at his keyboard again. "I've got a friend who's got a friend who happens to be a pirate. One who runs a lot of contraband across the Atlantic in his planes."

"What's it gonna cost?" Declan asked.

"More than we're willing to pay, but we don't have a choice." He opened an encrypted email server.

Jessie rushed to his side and batted away his left hand. "Let me do it. Just tell me what to say."

So he did.

"What about the summit?" Tessa asked. "I told my friend to notify those in charge, but he said they get threats like this all the time. They'll take precautions,"— she made air quotes—"but they won't call it off."

Meg stepped closer to the desk, her voice in mission mode. "Typical. They'd never have summits otherwise, though. There's nothing we can do for them at this point, unless we blow up the drone warehouse."

Dec pointed between himself and Meg. "So why don't we?"

One brow quirked at him. "Just the two of us?"

He nodded. "Tessa, Tommy—you two work with Spence and Jessie on Langley. If Brewer's got an entry point, you need to find it before he does while you're getting your asses back to D.C."

Jessie's jaw worked, clearly hating the division of labor but knowing they didn't have time to argue. "What if we're wrong?"

Spence looked up at her, eyes sharp but unreadable. "I know it feels like we're chasing our tails, but we'll get him, J."

She gave a short nod. "I promise to listen this time."

That earned another questioning look from Meg. "This time?"

"Not important," Spence said. His mail beeped. "This is my guy. I've secured us transport back to the States for a healthy sum of money and some very expensive rum. We leave Munich in an hour."

"Question," Tommy said, already grabbing his bag. "If Brewer's target is Langley, and the summit is just a smokescreen, then why is Hastings here? Why isn't he in D.C. already?"

Spence answered without hesitation. "Because Hastings doesn't give a rat's ass about Brewer. He's here to hedge his bets. That means he's holding something back. Something we can use."

"Or he's setting us up," Tessa said flatly.

"That too," Spence admitted. "Which is why we plan for every angle. No rushing in blind." He didn't look at Jessie, but knew she was taking that as a personal dig.

Dec's phone buzzed. He checked the message, then looked around the room. "We've got a three-hour window before the Berlin summit officially starts. Whatever we're going to do, we need to move now."

"Langley's got no idea what's coming. But we do," Spence said. "Let's make it count. We find Hastings, we find Brewer. And then, we end this."

TWENTY-ONE

Jessie

THE JET WAS the kind of ride politicians and CEOs used to cross oceans in comfort—cream leather seats wide enough to curl up in, brass trim on the fold-out tables, and a bar stocked with bottles that probably cost more than her monthly rent.

Soft lighting glowed from overhead, bathing the cabin in a gold warmth that didn't match the tight undercurrent of tension in her body. Spence, the mission, what they were heading into—they were all pushing her system into overdrive.

Their brief time on the couch replayed in her head over and over again. How it had felt to give in and act on their attraction. How it had gotten her out of her head for the first time in, what? A year?

Even now, she could feel his breath on her ear, his

skin on hers. The way his fingers probed, his lips lingered, his mouth tasted her...

The plane bounced on a wind current, and she snapped back to the moment. When Spence had said he had a pirate friend with a plane, she had assumed that they would be riding in a cargo plane filled with contraband. Never in her wildest dreams had she imagined such luxury. Even when she'd flown with Brewer in his private jet during her time with him, she hadn't experienced this level of glam. His jet had been impressive, but more calculated than comfortable. Apparently, the pirate business was lucrative.

And Spence had a very interesting past. Her mind ticked off all the things she now knew about him. About his mother and sister. His adopted father. His hunt for Victoria.

Her eyes tracked to him across the aisle, where he slept sprawled in one of the cushy chairs that tipped back. His six-foot-plus frame was just a bit too big for it, his injured hand cradled on his belly, while the other hung off the side. His feet dipped off the end of the padded leather footrest.

Exhausted. He was flat-out exhausted.

He'd fought sleep, just like he'd fought taking meds to relieve his wrist pain, but had finally given in when Tessa produced Percocet and insisted he take some. He wouldn't be any good to them once they landed if he was nursing his dominant hand, and something about the way she'd glared at him like a strict nurse in a hospital had stopped his argument before it passed his lips. Jessie had hidden her smile.

He'd reluctantly accepted the medication and, shortly afterward, fell asleep. Since he hadn't done so in at least two nights—even after what they'd shared on the apartment's couch—she was relieved to hear his light snores.

She tried not to think about the sex. The adrenaline letdown after the data center encounter, the close proximity while doctoring his hand, and their argument...

She scrubbed a hand over her face, losing the battle once more. The memories of his body, the rasp of his voice, the moment their walls cracked, and the fight between them burned into something else entirely, were on a repeating loop in her brain..

It was the source of her own insomnia at the moment, and why she was looking for a distraction, instead of watching his chest rise and fall, wanting to curl up next to him. All she wanted to do was keep a hand there, reassuring herself he was okay—safe for the moment in this plane high above a world under imminent threat.

A brutal shiver worked through her at that thought, also on replay. She forced her focus back to the laptop on the table in front of her, while outside the oval window, the Atlantic was an inky void, the thin line of the horizon barely visible against the night sky. They'd left Germany as the first rays of sunrise were lighting the sky and were now deep in darkness again as they winged home to D.C.

She should have been running down leads on Brewer, tracking his known aliases and allies within the

Maryland-Virginia area. If he'd partnered up with Hastings, there might be others with vendettas against the Agency whom he'd coaxed into his ranks.

Instead, her searches had drifted—Brewer's name still in the search bar, but the tabs multiplying with intel on Spence before she could stop herself.

His files were filled with info as well. Past missions, false IDs, operations with his name redacted so thoroughly she'd have better luck hacking the Vatican archives.

It was wrong to read his personal files. Unscrupulous and deceitful.

She did it anyway.

Because that frightened part of her that had been betrayed and manipulated too many times wouldn't stop.

Which made her feel like an awful partner. A terrible friend.

But oh, what she'd discovered about him. It only made her respect him more. In fact, she felt in awe of him and what he'd accomplished after what he'd survived.

They were both survivors. She'd known it before, but now, after what she'd read, it felt entirely different. She felt a deeper level of connection with him. Had a deeper understanding of what made him tick and why.

Flynn hadn't handed him the lead because of her and her issues—it had been *because of him.*

He'd been brainwashed to do whatever Ian Bastion wanted under the guise of protecting Britain at all costs. He'd been groomed and molded by the Mastermind into an agent before he ever became a soldier in the Queen's army or eventually an MI6 officer. He'd had his loyalty to the crown and his 'family' tested again and again.

And then found out it was all part of a secret shadow government.

The ultimate betrayal of his loyalty and allegiance. A betrayal of everything he'd valued.

She now understood the man she'd just opened up to in a whole different light. Understood his need to do the right thing. To prove he was the leader Flynn knew he could be.

He was the man she was falling in love with.

Jessie sensed movement in her periphery and glanced up to see Tessa sliding out of the seat next to Tommy's. The other woman crossed the aisle with the kind of quiet grace only an experienced operative could pull off—no wasted motion, no unnecessary sound.

Tessa eased into the seat across from her and tapped the laptop with a manicured nail. She was always stylish and put together, even when on a mission, and Jessie felt like a cretin next to her. "What are you working on? Brewer, I assume? I've been thinking of a multitude of ways to cut off his balls and torture him. Those are, of course, in line with the various ways I can kill him."

Jessie tapped a key to shrink one of the tabs and closed another casually. "Yep, just running a few searches to see if I can get a list of his U.S. allies or past coworkers who might also have a grudge against our employer. *If* we're still employed."

Tessa arched a brow, and the corners of her mouth curved in a way that was equal parts amused and sharp.

"Are you sure you weren't checking Spence's text messages and emails to see if he's involved with someone?"

Dammit. Tessa never missed anything. Jessie's cheeks heated. "Why would I do that?"

"He's not, you know. Involved with anyone. He hasn't had a relationship, even a casual one, in quite a while. In fact, I'd say, since he became a swan and fell head over heels for you."

It was no revelation. Jessie had known for a long time how Spence felt, but right now, the confirmation made her chest feel tight.

Tessa didn't back off. "It's not easy when certain emotions get tangled up with your mission, especially when you've been fighting them for so long. You two getting along okay?"

"Yes. No." Jessie huffed a faint laugh, pretending to focus on the trackpad. "Sort of. It's...complicated."

That earned her a knowing smirk—the kind that said Tessa had already guessed more than Jessie wanted to confirm. "Sex really complicates things on a mission. Add to the fact that he's the lead, and..." She flipped one hand back and forth. "Things could go either way for you in the emotional department, as well as with your career."

Tessa should know, considering that she and Tommy had given in to their attraction while chasing down Brewer six months ago. Their relationship had been tricky then, and still was, but their devotion to each other was rock solid.

Jessie snuck another glance at Spence. As messed up

as they both were, was it even possible for them to be rock solid?

Jessie's gaze slid toward her brother. He was leaning back with his eyes closed, one arm draped over the armrest and into the seat Tessa had vacated, as if he were reaching for her even now.

"I'm glad he has you," she said quietly, fingers still idly scrolling through one of Spence's redacted files. "But it feels like there's a wall between us since..."

Tessa didn't miss a beat. "Since he found out you weren't dead—and that you were working with Brewer."

Jessie's throat tightened. She gave a slight nod, closing one more tab before it could betray how deep she was digging. "Yeah."

Tessa's voice softened, but it didn't lose its conviction. "He knows you did it to protect him. All of us. He's not holding a grudge."

Jessie wanted to believe that. But wanting to believe it and actually believing it were two different things.

Her eyes drifted to Spence again across the aisle, head tipped slightly back, dark lashes resting against his tan skin. The laptop in front of her hummed softly, some of his world, his secrets, still open under her fingertips. "That's what I'm trying to do for him." She only wished she could make him see that. "He and the rest of the swans know Brewer to an extent. They know what we've faced and what's in the files, but they don't know him like you and I do."

Tessa's expression hardened. "And yet, he's still

outmaneuvered us. Outstrategized us. It makes me sick. It makes me feel stupid."

"Me, too. But here's the thing—it's not that he's brilliant, or more cunning than us. He's a psychopath with an ego. You once told him you could see his blind spots where he couldn't. I believe that's true. We've failed because we've been trying to outguess him. While you can see his blind spots, he can see ours. He knows our loyalty to the Agency is without question."

Tessa drummed her fingers on the top of the table, nodding as she caught on to what Jessie was thinking. "We have to stop being loyal soldiers. We have to be willing to break the rules to stop him."

Jessie sat back, relieved that they were on the same track. "You don't think I'm crazy?"

Tessa leaned forward and smiled. It was the smile of a predator who knew her next meal was only around the corner. "I think you're brilliant."

"I haven't been able to stop thinking about Flynn going off-grid and telling me before he did so to do *whatever it takes* to stop Brewer. It's like, he was giving me permission to turn everything on its head in order to bring down this madman."

"And you're worried the rest of the team won't back you up. Because they're still playing by the rules."

Jessie shrugged, her gaze flicking to Spence once more. "It's what we do. Sure, we skirt a few of the rules from time to time, but we are all loyal to the Agency and our country to a fault. And Brewer is counting on that."

Tessa's gaze sharpened, the predator-smile gone now,

replaced with something colder. More calculating. "Then maybe we stop playing by the rules altogether. He's playing chess while we've been playing checkers. If we're going to win, we take the board away entirely."

Jessie's pulse picked up. She'd been turning over the same idea since Berlin had first hit the radar. "We set our own trap."

"Exactly," Tessa said. "One he can't resist walking into."

They both glanced—instinctively—at Spence and Tommy, both still sleeping, oblivious to the fact that the two women across the aisle were quietly plotting a side op. Jessie's chest tightened at the thought of what either would say, but she forced her attention back to Tessa.

"It would have to be something Brewer can't delegate," Jessie murmured. "Something personal. Something that hits him where he's weakest, so he has to show up in person."

Tessa tapped the table again in thought. "And involve his ego."

Jessie's mouth curved in a humorless smile. "Yes. He has to prove he's the smartest one in the room."

They leaned in, voices dropping even lower as they sketched the rough outline—fake intel about a CIA breach only he could pull off, planted where they knew his people would find it. Layer it with just enough authenticity to make it irresistible. Dangle it like bait in front of a starving wolf.

"Codename?" Tessa asked.

Jessie didn't hesitate. "'Rat Trap.' Because when he

steps into it..." She closed Spence's laptop with a soft click. "...we slam it shut and make damn sure he never gets out."

Tessa's smirk returned, but this time it was sharper. "Now that's the Jessie I remember."

Jessie smiled back, but it was measured. "Let's just hope she's still good enough to pull it off."

In the back of her mind—where the doubts she didn't voice lived—she wondered what Spence would say when he found out. Would he see this as resourcefulness? Or proof she couldn't follow his lead? That thin thread of worry stayed there, coiled tight, even as she kept her gaze locked on Tessa and nodded like she was all in.

TWENTY-TWO

Spence

THE SAFE HOUSE was standard-issue two-story brick with blackout curtains drawn and a high-end security system. The place smelled of coffee and gun oil and was wired for secure communications.

It was close enough to Langley for a quick run if things went sideways, but far enough that the neighbors wouldn't notice the parade of "out-of-towners" coming and going at odd hours.

Spence sat at the dining table they'd converted into a war desk, his injured right hand braced on a gel pack while his left pecked at the keyboard. The others were scattered through the house—Jessie on the couch with another laptop from the supply chest of tech, Tessa cross-legged in an armchair scrolling through secure messages,

Tommy leaning against the kitchen counter sipping cold coffee.

His brain kept going through the same loop—Pentagon breach, drone warehouse, data center, Hastings, Brewer. Always back to the Pentagon. Always back to where this nightmare started.

Why?

The cursor blinked on a black terminal screen as Spence tunneled into a forgotten subdirectory on a Pentagon test server. He ended up on a Department of Defense server next, tracking remnants of Brewer's hack.

Maybe it was his insatiable need to follow every lead, or perhaps it was one of the tiny ways Brewer couldn't cover his tracks completely. But as he glanced down a list of files, one caught his eye.

CYCLONE: Test Log 546.

One folder. Locked.

His stomach dipped. A prickle ran up the back of his neck. *Cyclone.* That name didn't just belong to a project —it was his.

He read it again. And again.

CYCLONE: *Test Log 546.*

What were the odds this was tied to *his* cyclone?

Coincidence? Had to be, but...

He forced the encryption, bypassed two security rings, and when the file structure unfolded on his screen, the breath went out of him. Schematics. Build logs. Test footage. And there—burned into the firmware files like a scar—his encryption watermark. His work. His design.

They hadn't just stolen the design. They'd kept the name, like they didn't care about the theft.

Jessie's voice floated over from the couch. "What's that look?"

Spence's jaw flexed. He didn't answer, scrolling through frame after frame of his drones—only these weren't the stripped-down prototypes he'd mothballed. These were fully operational. Armored. Outfitted with modular payload cylinders exactly as he'd designed them to be.

Only now they'd been weaponized in ways the Pentagon had clearly spent years perfecting in secret.

Virus payload. EMP pulse. Thermal micro-charge. Armor-piercing microdarts. All loaded into a revolving chamber that could switch on command. Six kill methods in one drone.

He leaned back, the chair creaking. It felt like someone had reached inside his chest and twisted his heart. Then they'd done the same to his guts. "They built them," he said finally. "The project was supposed to be scrapped."

Jessie looked up. "Built what?"

"The Cyclones." His eyes stayed on the screen. "*My* Cyclones. Down to the last goddamn line of code."

No one spoke for a beat.

Tessa was the first to move, setting her tablet down. "Wait, those drone prototypes you built when I was still training recruits?"

He nodded, a fierce sense of betrayal burning a hole

right through him. "I suspected Brewer had gotten hold of my design, but I guess it's not him I should have been worried about. The U.S. has turned them into actual weapons after telling me the project was scrapped."

Tommy set down his mug. "You're saying—"

"I'm saying the Pentagon took my archetype and turned it into a fleet of fully armed, fully autonomous AI drones." Bitterness sharpened each word. So did incredulousness. "That's why Brewer wanted to breach the Pentagon's security. Not to test if he could. He was looking for already built weapons. And he hit the jackpot."

Jessie shifted to put her feet on the floor. "Holy shit. Are you sure?"

His guts roiled. "One hundred percent. The schematics are mine. The code is mine. They didn't even bother to alter it."

Tommy set down his cup. "What makes these drones different than others? Why are they valuable to Brewer versus the other high-tech weapons the Pentagon uses?"

He twisted his laptop so they could see the diagrams. "Like a six-shooter, each one comes with a revolving payload cylinder. Traditional military drones are mission-specific—one for recon, one for bombing, you get the idea. My design can pivot in seconds, switching from surveillance to attack to hacking without returning to base or swapping equipment." He rubbed his eyes. "Each drone's onboard AI can anticipate which payload to deploy based on real-time conditions—or override the operator entirely if programmed to. On top of that, they have a smaller profile than standard drones, making them harder to detect and track."

Everyone went still. The quiet that descended was too loud in his ears.

"Do you think Flynn had anything to do with it?" Jessie asked.

Had he? Had the director of Operations lied to Spence's face when he'd told Spence the program had been shelved because of the budget and other concerns with the tech? "You can bet that's the first thing I plan to ask him next time we talk."

"Give me the full scope of what these drones can do," Tessa said, all business. "What can the revolving cylinder carry?"

Because of her skills in design and layout, she was nicknamed The Architect. He appreciated her need for the specifics, even though it made his skin crawl to review the possibilities. "Possible payload types include micro-EMP disruptors, which can knock out electronics in a localized area without collateral infrastructure damage. Nano-virus dispersal canisters can release a cybervirus via micro-drones into targeted networks/devices from above, which are perfect for data center breaches. Precision explosives, small but devastating, can cause targeted destruction without leveling an entire building. Then there are recon/surveillance pods with multi-spectrum cameras, thermal, and LIDAR for mapping and tracking. Biochemical agent dispersal for crowd control. And finally, kinetic piercing rounds capable of shredding armored targets like vehicles or secure doors."

Again, that horrified silence fell. Yeah, this is what it felt like to be Dr. Frankenstein who'd created a monster. He couldn't look any of them in the eye. "The Pentagon has live versions, ready to be deployed. And Brewer wants them."

Jessie swore, putting her elbows on her knees and dropping her head into her hands. "If Brewer gets control of them to use on Langley…"

"The CIA won't stand a chance." He closed his eyes, sick to his stomach. "And I believe he's already got control or will have it soon. According to the project logistics, a whole fleet of them is armed and ready in a warehouse in Virginia."

They all shook their heads at the bad news that just kept on coming.

"He's never forgiven them," Tessa said, voice quiet and certain. "The CIA let him rot in prison. He expected a medal, or at the very least, a rescue." She slid the tablet aside. "He was a consultant in an unofficial capacity. Deep-level black ops. He trained agents, designed psy-op programs, and did worse. And never got credit for it."

Tommy added, "And he expected them to bail him out after he killed your mom."

Tessa's eyes were steel. "He thought the CIA was his gold card to do whatever he wanted. But when they let him go down for her murder, even if it was only manslaughter, he turned on them. Faked his death. Escaped. And has been slowly working his way back for his revenge ever since."

"And now he has the perfect weapon to do it," Spence muttered.

Jessie scrubbed a hand through her hair. "Okay, so what does that look like? Who does he go after?"

They were quiet again.

Tessa broke the silence. "The director?"

Tommy shook his head. "Too easy. Brewer thinks bigger. He wants to show the world what he can do."

Jessie nodded. "He's all about crippling infrastructure and systems. He'll go after their data, their agents, all of it. Expose everything and make them bleed with the world as his stage, watching."

Spence's pain was momentarily forgotten. "The Cyclones could be programmed to infiltrate the CIA's mainframe. They could fly into the building itself—into Langley—and deploy nano-viruses that wipe their databases clean or dump it all onto the dark web."

Tommy whistled under his breath. "Damn, man, when you design something brilliant, you go all out, don't you?"

"Public exposure is his goal," Tessa said grimly. "And that would do it. It would show the world what he can and will do, as well. He'll take full credit and bring this country, and plenty of others, to its knees."

"He might also cause a mass infection," Tommy offered. "Arm the drones with a biological agent. The drones release it inside the building, everyone breathes it in, then goes home and spreads it. He could infect half the Eastern seaboard if he times it right."

The drones can do all of that," Spence said, "and

more. Brewer's a sadist with a genius-level grudge. He won't stop at one payload—he'll deploy every option he's got."

Jessie's brows furrowed. "Wait a second." She snapped her fingers. "Flynn said something in his office the other day. He was answering emails and muttered something about an interagency review committee meeting being moved up because of the Pentagon breach. He said, 'Kill me now,' like it was the last thing he wanted to deal with."

Jessie rushed over to the desk, and her fingers flew over the keyboard. A second later, a schedule filled the screen. "It's behind closed doors, but it's not a secret. They have one every quarter. The CIA, Pentagon, Homeland, NSA, Feds, and certain White House staff convene to analyze some of the big, ongoing operations and discuss future ones. The long-term type of missions that involve multiple agencies and often span years, or even decades. They hold the meetings at different locations, and for this one, they're convening at Langley."

Tommy swore under his breath. "How the hell could Brewer find out about this?"

She shrugged. "Hacking a staffer's phone, hacking someone's calendar? Like I said, it's off books when it comes to the public, but everyone in these agencies knows about it."

"That's his moment," Tessa said, nodding. "It would be the most devastating attack on U.S. intelligence since 9/11. He'll make history."

Jessie straightened, her whole body tense. "And he'll

watch," she added. "Up close and personal because that's what gets him off."

"When is the meeting?" Tommy asked.

Jessie peered back at the screen. "Today. Fifteen hundred hours."

Three o'clock. Spence went cold. "We've got less than five hours to stop him."

TWENTY-THREE

Jessie

THE SAFEHOUSE CRACKLED WITH TENSION, even in silence. The team had spread out again. Tommy stood by the kitchen island, arms folded and brow furrowed. Tessa was seated near the window, scrolling through intercepts on her tablet. Spence paced behind the dining table, his boots thudding softly on the hardwood, his injured wrist cradled against his chest.

On the screen in front of her, Jessie scanned the Cyclone schematics, a digital autopsy of every spec, every payload chamber, every line of Spence's stolen code now potentially a weapon in Brewer's hands.

"No official Agency channels are gonna believe us in time if we try to warn them about the attack," Tommy said. "Even if they did, the minute they trace a call or ping back to us—"

"They'll think we're the ones planning something," Tessa finished grimly. "The Black Swan Division will be blamed for everything."

Jessie looked at Spence, who had stopped pacing. His expression was carved in stone, his eyes locked on his glowing screen, as if he were trying to rewrite reality by sheer will.

Her heart pinched. He looked devastated. Haunted. Like this betrayal was branded now into his DNA.

She knew what they felt like. How disempowered it made you feel. "Take them back," she said quietly.

Spence didn't move or even glance her way. "What?"

She set aside her tablet. "The drones. Brewer's only a threat if he has control of them. So take it back. Take control away from him."

Spence let out a rough sound—half scoff, half groan—and raked his good hand through his hair. "Once a system's been hijacked by someone like Brewer, it's not as simple as yanking out the batteries. Hastings' hackers probably already overwrote the operating parameters. Locked the original firmware out."

Jessie crossed her arms. "You're telling me there's nothing left? You didn't build in a backdoor? A failsafe? Something only you would know about?"

Spence's mouth opened to argue—then snapped shut. A flicker passed across his face.

Tessa and Tommy both stopped what they were doing to watch him.

Jessie felt a rush of hope. "You did, didn't you?"

Spence blinked, eyes narrowing as if mentally

zooming in on some dusty part of code he hadn't thought about in years. "During the prototype phase, I embedded a security override in the source kernel—a ghost protocol. It was never meant for production, just something I cooked up to test response thresholds in the field if we ever got to that phase."

Tessa scooted forward on the seat. "And Brewer doesn't know about it?"

"No one did. Not even Flynn or Del." Del was Flynn's favorite tech guru. "I encrypted it behind a misnamed string. Buried the trigger command in a fake boot error log."

Hackers and their signatures.

Tommy let out a breath. "Please tell me that's English for *we can use it now to stop this fucker.*"

"I don't know," Spence said, frowning. "Maybe. The Pentagon likely cloned the firmware before building anything. If the ghost protocol was in that version, and Brewer didn't spot it when he breached their security, then yeah. I might be able to force a reset. Trigger a kill switch that reverts the drones back to their original operating mode."

"And that will sever Brewer's control over them?" Jessie asked.

For the first time in the past twenty-four hours, he smiled. "It will revert control to me."

They all let out a collective breath.

She hated to ask, but had to. "And if it's not there?"

The flickering hope behind his exhaustion dulled. "Then we're screwed."

Jessie watched as Spence fully locked into figuring it out—fingers pecking one-handed while Tommy hovered over his shoulder, watching in awe. The screen was split four ways, decrypting firmware logs and tunneling through secure backdoors Spence had once built for himself and never shared with anyone.

God, he was brilliant. And clearly, this wasn't something she could help with. Not without slowing them down.

Perfect time for a covert Rat Trap errand.

She stood and stretched, making a show of wincing and cracking her neck. "I don't know about you all, but I'm starving. We passed a pub three blocks away—something McCallister's? I'm gonna run down and grab food."

Tessa's gaze flicked up from her tablet. She immediately caught the subtext. "I'll come," she said casually, standing and slipping on her jacket. "I need air."

Jessie slanted a look at Spence. "Want anything?"

He barely looked up. "Surprise me."

Tommy didn't even bother answering, which meant he trusted her to know what he'd eat. That, or he'd fully surrendered to caffeine and code.

Outside, the air was cool and damp—classic Virginia in early fall. The pub sat on a sleepy block that looked like Main Street USA, all brick facades and flower boxes in the windows. The sign over the door read McCallister's Public House – Est. 1939, and the scent of fries, burgers, and whiskey-soaked wood hit Jessie the moment they stepped inside.

She really was hungry. After they placed four orders

of the special to go, she and Tessa slid into a booth near the back, far from the early lunch crowd arguing about sports on the giant screen TVs all over the place.

"So," Tessa said, voice low. "What's our first move?"

Jessie glanced around, ducked her chin. "You ever seen Brewer panic?"

"Only twice. The night he killed Mom and realized the Agency wasn't going to cover for him, and then when we arrested him six months ago."

Jessie nodded. "Third time's a charm. Time to make him panic again."

"If he loses control of the drones, that should do it."

A waitress stopped and asked if they needed drinks while they waited for their order. Jessie thanked her but said no and waited for her to move on. "We need to up the pressure. Put a target on his back so big he can't move in public without setting off alarm bells."

Tessa frowned. "How?"

Jessie discreetly pointed at the nearest TV screen, where a news channel was on mute. A red ticker ran along the bottom with the day's highlights. "We go to the press."

Tessa smirked. "I like it."

"Our government has been trying to hide and cover up everything Brewer's been doing, so we flip the script. We expose him to every media outlet we can find. Makes it a hell of a lot harder for him to hide."

"Damn, girl. Talk about breaking the rules." She interlaced her fingers on the top of the table. "Where do we start?"

"We leak a falsified wanted bulletin with a Homeland or CIA logo on it. Make it appear as if it was extracted from an internal message and leaked to a whistleblower. It clearly states that Brewer is planning a domestic terrorist attack using drone warfare, that he was last spotted where Meg saw him, and it includes the most recent photos of him. The report hints at a connection to recent cyber breaches. We toss in buzzwords like EMP attack, nano-viruses, biochemical agents, whatever."

"Fear sells."

Jessie tapped the top of the table, keeping an eye on the nearby patrons, all absorbed in their food and beer. "Brewer will freak. He'll realize he's lost his precious drones and he's been outed as an imminent threat to the country."

Tessa expanded on it. "Best-case scenario, he gets arrested or ID'd before he can launch any plan against Langley, even if he has a backup outside of the drones. Law enforcement will be hunting him, throwing off his timeline and routes. Worst case, he has to scramble and pivot entirely. Either way, he'll be distracted and panic, which is where we come in and take him down."

Jessie pulled out her phone and began editing a memo from an old template she'd saved years ago for infiltration practice. Tessa typed notes into hers as they continued to chat—buzzwords, fear triggers, headlines she knew would get traction.

By the time their order was packed and they'd paid, they had finalized the text.

On the walk back, Tessa was already mocking up a

thumbnail for a video. "I'm fabricating a CIA-style classified video using media footage, internal jargon, and doctored images of Brewer's Pentagon breach. Want me to use his real face or the last alias we confirmed?"

Jessie thought about it. "Both. Split screen. Tag it with one of his old code names—Wraith. He used to say that a lot when I was with him and he was dealing with black market dealers. That'll make the dark web take notice. Throw in phrases he hates, triggers that will infuriate him. Include an AI-generated voiceover, deepfake style, from a 'government insider' saying they fear the CIA is covering it up."

Within minutes, Rat Trap was ready to launch. Back at the safehouse, Spence was still glued to his laptop, and Tommy had traded coffee for beef jerky.

Jessie dropped a greasy paper sack in front of each of them. "Eat."

Neither looked up, but both dived in. Jessie helped Spence with his order of fish and chips, removing the lid from the tartar sauce. Finally, he glanced up at her and smiled. It was tired, but it was real.

She leaned in and kissed his forehead.

Across the room, Tessa slid into her spot with a soda and a grin. When Jessie sat at the dining table across from Spence, she read a message from her.

The trap is set. Phase Two drops in ten.

Jessie downed her food, picking at her fries as Spence muttered lines of code under his breath like incantations. Tommy sat beside him, tracking progress on a parallel system, tapping in real-time intel from the black-market forums the CIA had been monitoring since Brewer had ghosted them six months ago.

Spence muttered more under his breath. "I buried the failsafe in the original Cyclone OS. It was designed to trigger if the drones were ever overridden by an external source—government or foreign. I hardwired a priority conflict line. If I activate it, every drone in the system flags its current controller as a hostile interface and drops into a fallback protocol."

Jessie muched on her last fry. She was still hungry. For food and for revenge. "And Brewer won't notice?"

"Oh, he'll notice. That's the point." Spence shot her a dry look. "He needs to realize he's no longer in control—believe someone else has wrested the drones from him. That's the bait. This way, he has to come to the site to try and take them back."

Tessa's brows hit her hairline. "A Pentagon site? Surely he wouldn't be stupid enough to take on a military compound."

Tommy grinned. "That's the beauty of it. The drones are being held at a private contractor site. Easier to hack into."

Spence pecked at more keys. "BIA Solutions. They've been on the government's payroll for years, and the warehouse is only ten miles from here."

Tommy's head snapped up. "Wait, I know that name." He tapped a fist against his head. "How do I know that name?"

Holy shit. The blood in Jessie's system froze.

"Brothers In Arms—BIA—it's one of Brewer's shell companies."

"Yes!" Tommy pointed at her. "I did that deep dive on him back in London and dug up dozens of shell companies he hid behind." His fingers scrambled over the keys. "Why didn't this place get tagged when I turned in that report after he escaped?"

Her insides crawled like they did every time she thought about how many of those shell companies she'd helped set up. "The place must have already passed inspection before you turned in your report and been greenlighted for the private contractor lists. Those lists are classified, so general analysts and Langley's computer bots don't have access to them. It didn't get tagged because it doesn't show up in any of the main databases."

Tommy threw up his hands and sat back. "That's why I do all of my own stuff. I should have followed up on it myself."

Spence waved a fry in the air before jamming it into his mouth and speaking around it. "Water under the bridge. We need to stay focused. Put our bait out there. The fact that he owns the warehouse actually helps us."

"How?" Jesse asked.

"He has more to lose, and he'll feel more confident, since he's in control of the security. We use that to our advantage."

Jessie wanted those words to reassure her. They didn't. "How are you making it look like the takeover is coming from the dark web?"

"Using one of his favorite haunts—Orchid Obsidian."

He nodded toward a terminal window. "It's one of his preferred hunting grounds. Shadow contracts. Illegal tech forums. Sometimes mercenaries post surveillance footage and tag code samples to flex."

Tap, tap, tap. Spence's concentration was locked in. "I'm uploading a forged command line breach right now, timestamped to show that someone using a handle called GhostKnife is cracking his control feed."

"Is that your alias?" Tessa asked from across the room.

He smirked. "Was. In my MI6 days. No one's used it in years, but enough old dogs remember it. Either way, the wanker's going to freak."

Tommy leaned in. "What if he thinks it's you?"

Spence's smile dropped. "Then he shows up extra pissed, which is exactly what I want."

Jessie watched the cursor flash, her nerves winding tighter. This was the equivalent of poking a dragon in the eye and hoping it flew into your trap instead of torching the village.

Spence hit *Enter.*

A soft tone chimed. The system had updated. Tommy tapped keys and watched the readouts flutter on his screen. "Looks good," he said. "Should see this on the forums in minutes."

Spence leaned back, exhaling hard. He grabbed Jessie's hand and squeezed.

From her perch across in the living room, Tessa gave Jessie a thumbs-up. Rat Trap had also just been executed.

She forced a smile at both of them. *Please, God, let this work.*

TWENTY-FOUR

Spence

IT DIDN'T WORK.

While he'd managed to bypass the warehouse's online security system and hack into the control hub, the Cyclones were not online.

Not with that hub.

Spencer dropped his head into his hands and swore. "Change of plans."

The three members of his team gathered around him. Jesse peered over his shoulder at the screen. "What's wrong?"

He hated the fear in her voice. The dread. He wished he could wipe it away with what he was going to say next. He couldn't. "The cyclones are on a local hub only."

"What does that mean? "Tessa asked.

Tommy let go of a flurry of curses under his breath

and whirled away. "It means we can't access them unless we are on site."

Jesse straightened. "Are you kidding?"

Spence dropped his hands into his lap and shook his head. "The only way for me to activate the failsafe is to go to the warehouse and hack into the separate control hub that Brewer has set up." He rubbed his eyes. "Bastard. Of course, he set it up this way. I would've done the same thing."

One of their phones let off a chirp. "That's mine," Tessa said, scrambling back to her chosen chair. She held it up and flashed the screen at them. The readout said 'Solomon.' Flynn's codename back when he was an agent.

Tessa hit the answer button and put it on speaker, returning to the dining room table and setting it down. "Hello, sir."

Flynn's voice came through low and taut. "We've got a situation. Hastings is inside Langley."

Jessie sucked in an audible gasp. "He survived the data center explosion?"

Spence rubbed his eyes again as he listened to Flynn drop the next bomb on them. "He's taken the director and multiple senior staff members hostage."

Another gasp from Jessie. Tommy swore vividly once more. Spencer's guts clenched hard. Tessa put her hand to her mouth and walked away from the table.

"We knew it was possible," Spence said. "But for the love of the Queen, we can't catch a damn break."

Flynn's next words made it worse. "He walked in

disguised as a DoD courier, shot two guards, and barri-caded the ops wing. He's demanding to speak directly to me."

Spence didn't need to guess why. Hastings had been, and maybe still was, Brewer's right hand, and both of them knew how to play the game. Was this another distraction? Was Hastings operating on his own? Or had this been part of the big plan all along?

Spence's pulse picked up, a too-loud drum in his ears. "Then you need to know this—the DoD took my Cyclone drone prototype and created a warehouse full of them. They're stored at BIA Solutions, ten miles from our safehouse. BIA is one of Brewer's shell companies. In essence, he has access to hundreds of deadly drones carrying payloads that could wipe out everyone and everything along the Eastern seaboard."

A beat of silence on the line. "The Cyclone project was shelved."

"Yeah, so we thought, but guess what? Someone lied, and Brewer is planning an attack on Langley as we speak *with those drones*. I need to get to his control hub. We take that hub, we cripple his ability to activate them."

Flynn's tone hardened. "We don't have time for detours. I want all of you at headquarters now. The hostages come first."

"That's exactly what Brewer's counting on," Spence said, leaning forward over the table, jaw tight. "You're asking us to walk into a kill box while he sits in a ware-house pulling the trigger."

Jessie was nodding beside him. "He's right, sir. If

Spence can get into the hub and upload his failsafe, Langley won't have to dodge an aerial strike in the middle of a hostage crisis."

Flynn swore under his breath, weighing it. "You're certain you can take control?"

"If I can get on site." Spence stared at this screen, wishing he had better answers. "I left a failsafe in the plans. I believe it's still there, but I can't access it remotely."

Another pause. Then Flynn made the call. "Fine. Swans three and four—you go to the warehouse. Five and six, meet me at Langley."

The line went dead, and Spence pushed away from the table. "Gear up, folks. The clock's ticking."

THE TWO-LANE BACK road cut through flat stretches of scrub and sagging chain-link, the kind of nowhere in rural Virginia that looked like it hadn't seen daylight in weeks. Spence kept the speed just under reckless, one hand on the wheel, his injured hand resting on his thigh as the odometer ticked them closer to BIA Solutions.

Industrial skeletons rose on the horizon—truck yards, half-dead warehouses, a grain silo tilting toward collapse. Somewhere in that maze of corrugated steel and asphalt sat the Cyclones' nest.

Jessie's voice had taken on the kind of tone that happened when adrenaline started to sharpen every thought and movement. Her focus was on the map on her tablet. "South fence line looks like our best bet. It's closest to where the service bays back up to the main floor. If we can get over without tripping the perimeter sensors, we can hug the shadows until we reach the catwalks above the control hub."

"Hub's not marked on the interior schematics," Spence said, eyes still on the road, "but it's always the same. It will be an isolated room with its own cooling system. Look for extra venting on the roof. That'll be our landmark."

She nodded, then glanced over at him. "You're mentally working on twelve strategies, aren't you? Because you're sure this is all going to go wrong."

"It's called planning," he said.

"It's called blaming yourself," she countered, softer now. "This isn't on you, Spence. The Pentagon stole your work. Brewer's the one using it against us."

He tightened his grip on the wheel. "Doesn't matter who started it. I'm the only one who can stop it."

A lie. It did matter. To him, anyway. He'd meant those drones to help people, especially the military personnel in the field. They were supposed to carry medicine and other tactical aid. Instead, they've been turned into horrifying weapons.

The silence stretched until the road curved and the industrial park's fence lines came into view, a jagged silhouette. Jessie leaned forward, scanning. "Target in sight."

Spence coasted the SUV into the shadow of an abandoned loading dock. From here, BIA Solutions sat like a crouched beast. Two stories of corrugated steel were wrapped in razor wire, floodlights on swivels, and a fence line humming with enough voltage to fry a man stupid enough to touch it.

He slid the binoculars from the dash and scanned the perimeter. Two guards in tactical black paced a lazy loop inside the fence, rifles slung but hands never far from their grips. Cameras rode the corners, angling in slow sweeps.

Jessie was already out of her seat, crouched against the SUV's hood as she adjusted her own optics. "South fence line's blind spot's smaller than I thought. Between the camera sweeps and patrol timing, we've got maybe eight seconds to cross open ground."

"Plenty of time," Spence said, though he clocked the math twice in his head. One missed beat and they'd be a flashing neon sign in the open.

She lowered her binoculars and returned to her seat before pointing to the roof. "If the control hub's got its own cooling system like you said, it's over there." The finger dropped to the section of the building directly below it. "That's where it'll be."

"And the server racks are usually in the heart of the operation," he said.

She watched the guards again through her binoculars. "It's going to be a bitch to get to them unnoticed."

Spence's jaw set, and he squeezed her shoulder. If only he could knock her out and leave her behind. Do this all on his own. But he couldn't. And he knew the importance of teamwork. "Then we plan on being noticed."

"I've got your back," she said, patting his hand on her shoulder.

"And I've got yours."

She leaned over and kissed him. Slow, sweet. For a second, he closed his eyes and let all thoughts fly away so he could enjoy it.

It might be the last time.

As she broke the kiss, the clock in his head started ticking down again. He cleared his throat, and they exited the car together.

At the guard change, Spence signaled Jessie forward, both of them sliding from cover into the cloudy afternoon light. The fence hummed like an angry hornet, the smell of diesel teasing his nose.

They kept low, moving along the shadows of a stacked pallet wall until they hit the south line. The nearest camera swept right.

"Now," he breathed.

Jessie went first—fluid, silent. In three steps, she was at the fence, cutter in hand. The insulated jaws bit through the chain-link. She peeled it back just enough to slip inside, her movements fast but unhurried, every inch the pro she was trained to be.

Spence followed, sealing the cut behind him with a magnetic clamp to hide the breach for as long as possible.

The guard patrol was late, which should have been a gift. Instead, it set his instincts buzzing. Too many ops had taught him lateness meant something else was already in motion.

Jessie dropped to a crouch and hugged the wall of the warehouse. She raised her gun as the soft crunch of boots on gravel approached from the east.

She didn't wait for Spence's nod. She flowed forward, intercepting the guard like a shadow. His expression never changed as she hit him with the barrel of her gun and eased him down to the ground.

Spence stepped over the unconscious body, resisting the urge to glance back. The soft glow of sodium lights painted the metal siding ahead as if it were night.

They were inside the perimeter. The hard part was about to start.

The loading bay loomed ahead, corrugated steel doors shuttered tight. Spence tucked in beside the keypad, fingers flying over the portable decryptor clipped to his belt. A soft chirp confirmed the bypass.

The door began to rise—just enough for them to slip under—when the afternoon quiet shattered.

"Contact, south bay!" The shout echoed across the yard, followed by the whipcrack of automatic fire. Bullets punched sparks from the bay door inches from Spence's head.

Jessie shoved him inside. "We're burned!"

The klaxon wailed to life, a gut-punching blast that rolled through the warehouse like an air raid. Red strobes began to pulse along the walls, bathing everything in a hellish glow.

Inside, the space yawned wide—rows of steel

shelving stacked high with crates, the tang of machine oil and ozone in the air. Overhead, catwalks spiderwebbed across the expanse, and far at the opposite end, a glass-walled room glowed faint blue. The control hub.

Two guards barreled out from behind a forklift, rifles up. Spence fired first, the suppressed shots coughing in the cavernous space.

One went down. Jessie was already moving on the other, kicking the rifle away before he could bring it to bear.

"Go!" she barked, hauling Spence forward.

He sprinted for the cover of the nearest crate stack. Boots thundered above on the catwalks, shadows criss-crossing in the strobe light. The sound of more incoming fire rattled the metal walls.

They moved like they'd trained for this—because they had. In the early days of the swans, they'd gone through mock scenario after mock scenario before they ever went into the field as a team.

Jessie swept left, taking the aisle along the forklift line, while Spence advanced up the right, using the crate stacks as cover. Gunfire ricocheted off steel and concrete, sparking like welding torches in the strobe light.

Above, boots pounded the catwalk. Muzzle flashes strobed in return, raining rounds that chewed splinters from the crate corners. Spence ducked, heart hammering in rhythm with the klaxon, and sent two clean shots upward. One guard dropped screaming, his rifle clattering against the rail before disappearing into the shadows below.

They closed in on the hub. Fifty meters. Forty. Jessie caught his eye, signaling with two fingers—two hostiles ahead. He nodded, pivoting around a crate corner just as she flanked the other side.

A double-tap from him. A brutal elbow strike from her. Both targets were down.

They pushed forward, their boots hitting the polished concrete in quick, efficient strides—until the overhead PA crackled.

"Well," a voice drawled, rich with mockery and familiarity. "If it isn't the prodigal daughter and her plus-one."

Spence froze. He knew that voice.

Brewer.

"You've got good timing," the man continued, his voice echoing through the warehouse. "I was wondering how long it would take you to find my little toy chest."

Jessie shot Spence a look—half fury, half warning—and motioned toward the hub. But Spence couldn't stop the ice creeping into his veins. Brewer was *here*.

All the better to catch you, motherfucker.

The glass-walled room seemed to pulse brighter, like a beacon daring them to try. Between them and that door lay two more rows of crates—and God knew how many men waiting in ambush.

"Keep moving," Jessie muttered, reloading on the run. "I've got you covered. We're finishing this."

Spence swallowed his rising anger, shoved it down into something sharp and focused, and pushed on.

The glow of the control room was just ahead. A cube of frosted glass was elevated on a steel mezzanine, cables snaking from its base like roots feeding the entire facility.

Spence's pulse kicked into a higher gear. Almost there. He kept Jessie on his six as they cleared another row of crates, his pride over her not reacting to Brewer's comment about her being the prodigal daughter teasing at the back of his mind.

Then a slow, deliberate clap echoed off the corrugated walls.

Brewer stepped from the shadow between two forklift bays, flanked by two armed men. He wore that smug half-smile that made Spence's teeth ache to knock it off.

"Well," he said, "you two have been busy little bees." His gaze flicked to the control room above them. "Looking for this?"

Spence's grip on the rifle tightened. "We're taking them back."

Brewer's smile widened, predator amused at prey. "You think you're in time? Oh, Spence. You should know better than anyone—the Cyclones don't wait around for permission."

A cold weight dropped in Spence's gut. "What do you mean?"

"They lifted twenty minutes ago. Low and quiet in stealth mode and headed for Langley as we speak. By the time you two figure out how to work that console, they'll be circling like sharks over your precious Agency." Brewer tipped his head, mock thoughtful. "But I'm not without hospitality. I kept a few toys here. Wouldn't want my guests to get bored."

As if on cue, a high-pitched whir spun up above the din. Spence's heart lurched as two Cyclones swept from the shadows of the rafters, payload cylinders gleaming under the work lights.

Jessie muttered, "Son of a—"

"I'd better run along," Brewer said, stepping back into the dark as his men raised their rifles. "I've got the best seat in the house to watch you both die."

TWENTY-FIVE

Jessie

THE HIGH-PITCHED WHIR hit her ears a split second before the shadow dropped from the rafters. Two Cyclones swept into view, cylinders gleaming like loaded revolvers under the work lights.

Jessie's brain shifted into overdrive. They couldn't outgun both the drones and Brewer's men in the open. Spence needed to get to that control hub—the only shot they had at stopping the rest now on their way to Langley — and she needed to buy him that time.

She glanced at the catwalk ladders and the narrow gaps between the crates, mapping them in her head. Cover, height, distraction. There. That's where she'd station herself. She leaned toward Spence. "Go for the hub. I'll keep him busy."

His jaw flexed, eyes locking on hers. "Jess—"

"Do it," she cut in, already moving toward a stack of crates to draw fire. "You're the only one who can shut them down."

The drones' rotors screamed to life. Brewer stepped back into the dark, his voice floating after him. "Better hurry. Clock's ticking."

The drones split in the air, one veering high toward the control room windows, the other dipping low to lock onto her. Jessie swore under her breath. Brewer was covering both of them.

"Spence!" She ducked as the lower drone's micro-darts chewed into the crate edge. "Incoming!"

"Working on it!" His voice came from behind the reinforced glass, the frantic clacking of keys a counter-point to the rising pitch of the drones.

She pivoted around the crate, fired a double tap at the low drone, and managed to nick a rotor arm. The thing wobbled but stayed airborne. "Brewer's in the wind! I can't find him."

The high drone scraped across the control room glass, metallic claws sparking as it tried to chew through the pane. "I've got the port open," he called. "I just need thirty seconds."

Thirty seconds in a firefight might as well be thirty years.

Movement flickered in her periphery. *Gotcha*.

Brewer was on the catwalk, closing in on the control room with a compact SMG slung at his side. His smile was tight and cold, eyes fixed on Spence's back.

Not happening.

Jessie popped up and fired at Brewer. He jerked aside, the round grazing the rail instead of his ribs, but it forced him into cover.

The low drone banked again, payload cylinder clicking into thermal charge position. Her stomach clenched. If it fired that in here, half the warehouse would light up like a tinderbox.

But her next thought calmed her worry. Brewer would never do that to his own warehouse. It was just for show, and she knew it.

"Jessie, down!" Spence barked.

On reflex, she dropped as he triggered something on his end. The drone above her seized midair, rotors shrieking, then crashed to the floor in a shower of sparks.

Yes! One down.

Brewer was moving again, using the distraction to close the gap. The second drone had switched to EMP mode and slammed against the control room window. Brewer needed to cut power to Spence's console before the upload finished.

It was up to her to stop it.

Jessie bolted from cover, crossing the open floor under a hail of SMG fire from Brewer. Pain lanced through her shoulder—hot, sharp, and deep—but she didn't slow.

She hit the control room door, threw herself inside, and slammed the lock. "Finish it," she ground out, pressing her hand over the wound.

Spence's jaw was set, eyes locked on the progress bar crawling toward completion. "Almost there."

Brewer's voice came muffled through the door. "You think you can stop me, Stirling? You're just handing me proof you're the only one who can control them. And I'll take that from you the same way I take everything else."

Jessie drew her sidearm, moved to the glass. Pointed at him. "Try it."

The bar hit one hundred percent. Spence hit ENTER. The drone dropped like a stone.

But Brewer's smile through the glass told her this wasn't over. Jessie froze when he held up a phone, the screen tilted just enough for her to see the shaky, bird's-eye feed of Langley's sprawling campus. The image swayed as the drone whose feed she watched banked, the sun flashing off its wing.

Her heart slammed against her ribs. Tommy. Tessa. *God, please...*

"Destruction's already a certainty," Brewer said, voice slick with satisfaction. "No matter what you do, you won't stop them all."

"Not all," Spence muttered beside her. His jaw was locked, eyes on his screen. "But I can knock some out of the sky."

A sharp tone chirped from his system. A third of the feed cut to static.

Brewer's head snapped toward the monitors, fury tightening his mouth. "Cute trick." His gaze slid to Jessie, and the anger melted into a mocking smile.

"You disappoint me, Jess." His voice dropped into that intimate, snake-oil tone that had once convinced her to follow him into hell. "I had big plans for you. You could've been standing here beside me when the world watched the CIA burn. Instead, you're running errands for the people who betrayed you."

Her grip on her gun tightened. "Better than rotting in your shadow."

Brewer chuckled, but the sound didn't reach his eyes. "Where's your brother, Jess? Safe at home? Or about to be a smear on the pavement when the first payload hits?"

She refused to give him the satisfaction of flinching. "You can't manipulate me anymore."

On the screen in his hand, the drone's live feed flickered. Rows of Cyclones tumbled out of formation, spiraling toward the ground like metallic hail. "It's working," she muttered to Spence. "Whatever you're doing, it's working."

Brewer narrowed his eyes, not seeing the show.

She tipped her head, letting a slow smile curl on her face. "Looks like you're losing this one, Brewer."

Brewer's smile froze. He narrowed his eyes. The live feed on his phone jolted, the frame stuttering before the horizon tilted wildly. More rows of matte-black drones tumbled from the sky like dead birds, slamming into rooftops and asphalt in puffs of dust and debris. The one streaming the feed juddered midair, then went black.

She pointed at the screen. "Look."

His gaze snapped to the phone, and for a heartbeat, she thought she saw the truth under his polished mask. Not rage or disappointment. Humiliation.

"You," he hissed, voice cutting through the partition as if it could carve her open. "Always ruining what you don't understand." His hand curled so tightly around the phone she half expected the screen to crack.

Jessie didn't take her eyes off of him, even as Spence hissed and groaned. This was a victory...what was wrong? She didn't dare take her eyes off Brewer, though. "I understand you better than you think."

His eyes flared, cold and bright, and the mask snapped back into place. It was stretched too tight now, trembling around the edges. "This changes nothing," he snarled. "Langley will still burn. And when it does, you'll wish you'd taken what I offered you."

TWENTY-SIX

Spence

THE UPLOAD BAR was at seventy-eight percent when every monitor in the control room blinked once, then died.

Black screens.

Dead silence.

Spence's stomach dropped. "Son of a—"

Brewer had shut down the hub's power, stopping the failsafe activation before it could finish. The bastard had cut him off at the knees.

Through the glass partition, he saw Brewer heading for the rear of the warehouse, his long coat snapping behind him.

"Jessie!"

"I see him!" she shouted, barreling after the man.

Spence shut his laptop and shoved it in its sling,

grabbed his weapon, and ignored the screaming protest in his injured hand as he bolted after them both.

They burst into the main warehouse floor, a cavern of shadows and sharp angles. Forklifts loomed like sleeping beasts, their forks jutting up like steel tusks. Towering stacks of drone crates formed narrow aisles, each one a choke point waiting to be used against them.

Jessie was just ahead, moving like a ghost between the rows of crates, her boots barely making a sound. Brewer scrambled past a tool area, glanced back once, and fired a quick burst over his shoulder. Jessie dove behind a forklift. The alarm klaxon continued to wail overhead, a bone-deep howl that set Spence's teeth on edge.

He cut left, angling to flank Brewer, catching brief flashes of him going up a catwalk, down again, moving in unpredictable bursts that forced them to adjust course constantly. Brewer knew this place's layout better than anyone, and he was using it to bleed time off the clock.

A forklift chain clanged as Brewer brushed past, vanishing behind a stack of crates. Spence's pulse roared in his ears. Every second Brewer stayed ahead was another second the second fleet of drones got closer to Langley.

Jessie shot him a quick look over her shoulder. "We can't let him get out through the rear bay door."

"Let's cut him off," Spence said, breaking into a sprint.

They rounded the end of a crate stack—and ran straight into Brewer's ambush.

Gunfire ripped through the narrow aisle, splintering wood and pinging off forklift steel. Spence dropped behind cover, dragging Jessie with him. Her shoulder slammed into a crate, and she yelped through her teeth, but she was already returning fire.

Brewer fired two shots, shifted, fired off two more, keeping them pinned while edging closer to the loading bay.

Spence spotted his opening near a catwalk ladder and broke left, using the angle to try to duck under it and box the man in. He caught Brewer before he got to the bay, and for the first time, Spence saw his calm crack. Their eyes met over the sights of their weapons.

"You just don't know when to quit, do you?" Brewer yelled, voice carrying over the ringing in Spence's ears.

"Funny," Spence shot back, "I was about to say the same to you."

Brewer's smirk twisted into something cruel. Something that reminded Spence of Ian Bastion at the end, when Spence and his two step-brothers had had the man cornered. Brewer opened his mouth to say something, but Spence wasn't interested in hearing it. He squeezed the trigger.

Brewer pivoted, taking the bullet in his arm. He disappeared behind a group of barrels.

Jessie stalked up from the other side, weapon trained on the spot. Spence waved her off, and then had to whirl around when he heard footsteps coming from behind him.

The shot by the guard went wide. Metal screamed as it ricocheted. Spence fired and the guard went down.

"Spence!"

Jessie's voice was an octave too high. He ducked, spinning at the same time, and a bullet whistled over his head.

Then Brewer was there, right in front of him. Spence brought up his weapon, but Brewer knocked it aside with his own.

The bastard was strong, and Spence's hand was screaming. He tried to leverage Brewer's momentum into a takedown, but Brewer rolled with it, forcing him back toward the crates.

The muzzle came up, this time steady on Spence's heart.

Spence's pulse spiked. He saw the twitch in Brewer's fingers—the tiny, inevitable squeeze that meant this was it.

"Look out!" Jessie came out of nowhere, slamming into Brewer's side. The shot cracked like thunder in the enclosed space. Pain lanced across Spence's ribs—not his pain. Her weight hit him hard, her knees buckling as they went down together behind a forklift.

"J!"

Her breath hitched, eyes wide but fierce. Blood bloomed hot against his hand where he clamped over her side. "You idiot," she rasped, forcing a smirk that didn't hide the tremor in her voice. "You're not dying on my watch."

"Dammit, Jess—" His throat was tight, rage and fear tangling until he could barely see straight.

Across the aisle, Brewer raced toward the loading bay.

Spence started to rise, torn between going after him and keeping pressure on the wound, but Jessie's grip on his jacket stopped him. Her fingers curled in the fabric, holding him there with more strength than she should've had.

"Finish it," she whispered, blood staining her teeth. "Take him down."

He shook his head. "I'm not leaving you."

Her eyes softened, a rare crack in her armor. "I love you, Spence."

It was a sucker punch straight to his chest. He swallowed hard, forcing a grim smile even as his hand stayed pressed to her side. "Then don't make me live without you. Got it?"

The echo of Brewer's footsteps faded, punctuated by the slam of the loading bay door. Somewhere out there, the bastard was slipping into the dark, carrying whatever fight he had left straight to Langley.

Spence's muscles screamed to go after him and finish this. Every instinct drilled into him through years of ops screamed *move, chase, kill*.

But Jessie's blood was warm against his palm, and dammit, there was too much of it. Too, too much.

He swore under his breath and scanned the shadows, listening for a second wave of gunmen. Nothing yet, but he knew they'd come.

"We can still—" She tried to push herself up, but the effort wrung a sharp cry from her throat.

"Don't," he said, more harshly than he meant. His free hand found her cheek, tilting her toward him. "We're not doing the hero bleed-out thing, Agent Medoza. That's a direct order."

"Spence—"

"Not negotiable." He shifted, hauling her arm over his shoulders and forcing her to her feet. She stumbled, but he caught her, keeping his injured hand clamped to her side as they moved.

Each step was a calculated retreat, weaving them back through the maze of crates toward the catwalk stairs and out of the line of sight from the bay.

He could still picture the drones screaming toward Langley. But right now, the mission wasn't a fleet of Cyclones or stopping Brewer in his tracks. It was Jessie.

And no one—not Harris Brewer, not the Pentagon, not even the CIA—was going to take her from him.

"I should have shot him," she mumbled, "but I was afraid I'd hit you."

He half-carried, half-dragged her through the warehouse's side exit, his arm locked around her waist, her blood soaking into his shirt. The night air was damp, cold, and smelled faintly of diesel from the truck yard beyond. "And then you took a bullet for me. Such a dick move, Mendoza."

She grunted a laugh. "Told you to stay out of the field."

They reached the SUV, and he eased her into the

passenger seat, shoving his pack onto her lap. "Keep pressure here," he ordered, tearing open a field dressing with his teeth. His injured right hand was slow and clumsy, but he wrapped her side as tightly as he dared.

"Call Tommy," she rasped.

"That's not the most important thing here."

Her eyes were glassy but fierce. "Call him. I need to know my brother's okay."

"Taking care of you is my priority."

"Damn it, Spence—"

He cursed under his breath, snatched his phone from his pocket, and stabbed Tommy's number with his thumb. The kid picked up, and Spence said, "Talk."

"Drones are down," Tommy said without preamble. "Langley's secure. Hastings is—"

"Neutralized?"

"Yeah. You guys okay?"

Spence tightened the last knot in her bandage. "On our way to Walter Reed. Meet us there."

"What?"

"It's nothing," Jessie called out, her voice too thin to sell the lie. Spence ended the call before Tommy could ask them more questions.

He swung into the driver's seat, slammed the door, and dropped the gearshift into drive. The tires screamed as they tore out of their hiding place and onto the two-lane road.

Up ahead, headlights flared—Brewer's black sedan.

"Follow him," Jessie said, trying to sit forward.

"We're going the same way," he said, jaw tight.

She levered the rifle into her lap from the back seat. "Good." Before he could stop her, she had the barrel out of the open window. The crack of a shot split the night, the back window of Brewer's sedan exploded, and the car fishtailed hard.

"Jessie!" He grabbed the back of her jacket, yanking her inside as the sedan veered off the shoulder and plowed into a telephone pole.

"Stop!" She beat at his injured hand, and he nearly let go when pain erupted in his wrist all over again. "Arrest him!"

He accelerated and they whizzed past. "I'm not letting you bleed you out for an arrest."

Her hand slipped from the rifle, her body going limp. Her head lolled against the seat.

"Jessie." He shook her. But she was unconscious. "Dammit, woman."

He blew through two red lights and didn't slow until the gates of Walter Reed loomed ahead. Military police waved him through after a glance at his credentials and a look at Jessie, slumped in the seat, pale as chalk.

He skidded into the ER bay, yanked open her door, and had her in his arms before anyone reached them.

"GSW, left side," he barked as the trauma team rolled up with a gurney. "Through-and-through, but she's lost a lot of blood."

Hands were on her then, lifting her, cutting the bandage he'd tied. Someone shouted for more IV fluids. The doors swallowed her, leaving him standing in the wash of fluorescent light and antiseptic air.

His right hand throbbed like hell, his shirt was stiff with her blood, and he couldn't shake the sound of her voice in the warehouse—*I love you.*

He moved to follow, but a nurse barred his way. "You need to wait here, sir."

"She's—"

"They've got her," the nurse said firmly. "Let them work."

Spence turned away before he punched the wall. He braced both hands on the counter, forcing himself to breathe.

Ten minutes felt like ten years before Tommy appeared, Tessa right behind him.

"They said she's stable," Tommy reported, eyes flicking to the dried blood all over Spence. Flynn already spoke to the surgeon. "Are you...?"

"I'm fine." His voice was flat.

Tommy frowned. "The best surgeons are on it. She'll be okay."

Spence nodded, jaw tight, knowing Tommy was trying to convince himself as well as Spence.

Inside, he replayed every second between Brewer aiming at him and Jessie stepping into the line of fire. Tommy insisted he tell them everything, and he did, fighting to keep his cool, calculated self in place so he didn't punch a wall.

An hour ticked by, and when they finally wheeled her into recovery, her eyes cracked open just enough to find him.

"You didn't arrest him," she murmured.

He leaned down, his voice rough. "You didn't give me the chance, sweetheart. You were too busy taking bullets for me."

Her lips twitched with the ghost of a smile. "Told you... You needed me."

He brushed a strand of hair from her forehead. "Yeah. You're damn right I do. Now, stop talking and get some rest."

TWENTY-SEVEN

Jessie

THE FIRST THING she noticed was the smell—bleach and antiseptic. The second was the ache blooming from her shoulder, thick and dull under the heavy weight of bandages. The third was the soft beeping at her side, an IV drip snaking into her arm.

Jessie blinked at the ceiling tiles, blurry around the edges. Her throat was dry, her mouth like sandpaper. She turned her head, wincing.

Through the cracked bathroom door, she heard a voice.

Spence.

Low and tight, laced with exhaustion. "Understood. I'll file the report when we get clearance. Yeah. I couldn't be happier the bloke is dead."

A pause. Then, "Hastings is in custody?" His voice

lifted, incredulous. "I'll be damned. I figured he'd take out half the compound before he let you take him alive." A longer pause. "Roger that. See you in ten."

Jessie swallowed, her voice rasping against her dry throat. "Spence?"

The bathroom door flew open, and he appeared, dark circles under his eyes, his right hand in a soft brace, his phone in his other. Relief flooded his face as he crossed to her.

"You're awake." The look morphed into that steady, calm smirk that usually annoyed her. He clumsily poured water into a plastic cup with a straw. "About damn time, Swan Three. You don't usually slack off on the job like this. Of course, this is what happens when you take a bullet for your boss and then nearly fall out of a moving car."

She started to chuckle, but it hurt.

He held out the cup, placing the straw to her lips. His sarcasm left as quickly as it had come as she sipped. "God, J, you scared the hell out of me. On our next mission—if we get one—I'm securing you in bubble wrap."

The water was too good, soothing her parched throat. She sipped again, too fast, and coughed. "How long have I been out?"

"Eight hours." He set the cup on the rolling tray next to her bed and gently touched her forehead. "They got the bleeding stopped. You lost a lot of blood, but you're stable. No major damage, just a whole lot of pain meds and a pissed-off shoulder."

She tried to sit up—instantly regretted it.

"Whoa." He eased her back with a hand on her good arm. "Don't even think about playing tough right now."

Everything hurt, even with the meds they were pumping into her veins. "And Brewer?"

Please be captured. Please be captured. Please be captured. She couldn't stand the thought that he was still out there. That this had all been for nothing.

He sat on the edge of the mattress, expression serious but lighter, too. "He's dead. The impact with the pole crushed the entire front of the car." At her relieved sigh, he nodded and squeezed her hand. "He'll never hurt anyone again."

Thank God. "And Hastings?"

"In a cell. Tried to use a stolen access badge to get out of the sublevel—ran straight into Flynn and a half-dozen CIA HRTs." Spence gave a crooked smile that didn't reach his eyes. "Tessa said it was poetic."

Jessie exhaled heavily again, her shoulders relaxing into the bed. Everyone was okay. The bad guys were done. "And the drones?"

"They're down," he confirmed. "All of them. The failsafe worked. Pentagon confirmed a full blackout sweep."

His hand was warm and reassuring. So was the gentle smile he gave her. She could have lost him. Could have lost Tommy and Tessa.

But she hadn't, and in fact, may have regained part of her soul that she'd sold to Brewer a year ago.

She squeezed Spence's fingers with as much strength as she could muster. "You did it."

He looked at her like she was the only thing in the room worth seeing. "*We* did it. Partners, remember?"

"Forever?"

"On one condition."

She quirked a brow. "Just one?"

He snorted, then turned serious. "You promise not to go behind my back and make a plan with Tessa again that affects the mission, or our partnership."

"Oh, that."

"Yeah, that," he said, making a contrary face. "What were you thinking?"

"I wanted to put as much heat as possible on Brewer."

"I'm afraid he never saw any of it, but you sure riled up a whole lot of people."

"Including our boss?"

"Actually, just between us, Flynn laughed. He bitched out Tessa, of course, when she took credit for it, but he recognized your fingerprints all over Rat Trap. I expect you'll get an official slap on the hand when you go back to work, but secretly, I think he's pleased."

When I go back to work... Was she going back?

The question pinged around in her brain. What else was she going to do? She was a trained agent, not the girl next door. If the CIA still had a job for her, she'd take it, even if it was behind a counterterrorism desk again. As long as Spence was there, nothing else mattered.

She laced her fingers through his, her grip still weak

but sure. "Back at the warehouse, I told you something. I wasn't sure if you heard me."

His eyes darkened. "I heard you."

She swallowed, bracing herself. "I meant it."

He didn't look away, didn't deflect with sarcasm or distance like he usually did when things got real. His hand tightened around hers, thumb brushing along the inside of her wrist. "I've been in love with you since our first swan mission," he said softly.

The beeping monitor and the hall sounds faded away to nothing. She'd known he'd had feelings for her for a while, but not for *that* long.

"I didn't want to be," he continued. "You were reckless, opinionated, and way too good at pushing my buttons. And when I thought you were dead, only to discover you weren't..." His throat bobbed with the words he didn't say.

"I betrayed you," she whispered.

"You came back," he countered. "You chose to come back. You risked everything to stop Brewer. To protect your brother. To protect me."

The swans hadn't exactly given her a choice, but they hadn't had to push too hard to get her to cooperate.

She blinked against the sting in her eyes. "After everything I did, how could you still want me?"

"Because I know who you really are." His lips twitched with a sly grin. "You never run from a fight, and you've never stopped trying to make things right. You're stubborn and impulsive, but also loyal. To me, to your brother, to saving the world."

Tears slid down her cheeks. She didn't bother to wipe them away.

"You're it for me, luv," he said. "Always have been."

Her pulse seemed too loud in her ears, her body too warm under the sheet and coarse blanket. "You're going to make me believe in second chances, you know."

The grin grew, curving his lips. "I'm a firm believer in them. I've been given more than I deserve, and look how good I turned out."

He winked and she grinned through her tears. "We really need to work on bolstering your confidence."

Just as he brushed a hand over her hair, careful not to jostle her bandaged shoulder, a knock sounded on the closed door.

Before either of them could answer, it creaked open and Tessa poked her head inside, a wild spray of grocery store flowers in one hand and a suspiciously large bag of gummy worms in the other.

"Hope we're not interrupting," she said, grinning.

Jessie let out a tired laugh. It hurt, but she didn't care. "Get in here before I start crying again."

Tommy followed close behind, holding up a bottle of sparkling apple cider like it was champagne. "Vintage... uh, fifteen minutes ago. Courtesy of the vending machine."

Spence groaned. "If you pour that over my head, I swear—"

"Tempting," Tommy deadpanned, "but I'll settle for toasting the fact that we saved the world. Again."

Jessie smiled, soft and a little wobbly, as her brother

set the bottle aside and leaned in for a hug. It wasn't awkward—not anymore. It was solid. Real. The kind of hug that said *we made it* without needing to say the words.

She clung to him fiercely. "I thought I'd lost you."

"Not a chance," he said, gripping her just as tightly. "You're stuck with me."

Tessa dropped the gummy worms in Spence's lap and slid into the chair next to him. "Flynn's calling you both reckless geniuses."

Jessie raised a brow. "Both of us?"

Spence gave her a crooked smile. "You did take a bullet and shoot out Brewer's back window on the way to the hospital."

Tessa smirked. "Ballsy."

"Against my orders, I might add. I'm still mad about that," Spence muttered.

"You're welcome," Jessie said sweetly.

Laughter bubbled up. It was the first genuine laughter any of them had shared in what felt like forever. It settled in the air, light and warm. For the first time, the room didn't feel haunted by what they'd done or what they'd lost. Just who they still had.

Jessie glanced at Tommy, then at Spence.

Her brother was here. Alive. Hers.

And Spence was too.

TWENTY-EIGHT

Spence

THE HOSPITAL ROOM WAS QUIET, save for the soft blip of Jessie's monitors and the distant hush of a cart rolling past in the hallway. Spence sat in the corner chair, one ankle hooked over his knee. He'd tucked a blanket around Jessie's shoulders and now watched as she slept deeply, her face slack and peaceful for the first time in days.

But he was wide awake.

He'd had his wrist looked at and now sported an ugly brace. A bottle of pain meds sat nearby, but he didn't need them. He just needed her.

He kept one hand on the armrest, the other curled around the Queen Victoria shilling that had traveled with him since the night he'd stopped being a kid. Its edges were worn smooth, its inscription faded, but it had always tethered him to something...even if he never quite knew what.

Tonight, it felt like more than a memory.

He reached for his laptop, careful not to wake Jessie, and flipped it open. With a few keystrokes, he decrypted the file he'd stored back at the safe house. Staring at the strange string of letters and numbers, he knew he had to find the connection.

Vic609-bellcov-97firewatch

He ran it through everything. Search engines, archived intelligence reports, off-grid black ops archives. Nothing useful came up.

Until he added one word: London.

Suddenly, something pinged.

"Holy queen and country," he murmured. Bellcov wasn't a place—it was shorthand for Bell Covenant, a disused church turned shelter near Camden Market, where displaced children had sometimes ended up in the early nineties. He'd slept behind its crumbling steps a few times and still remembered its black bell tower, the fire-scorched bricks.

And Firewatch97? One of his databanks pinged again when he added the same term. London.

He gobbled up the info, mentally doing a palm slap when he found the details. It was an off-the-books security program created by MI5 for the protection of sensitive civilian witnesses. Used only in the most politically damning cases, ones that would unravel entire networks if exposed.

His pulse kicked up. He traced the memo trail until

he found a declassified fragment buried in a corrupted directory.

Asset Name: Victoria Marsh

Age: 6

Status: Relocated under Firewatch97 protocol

Reason for Custody: Witness to Operation Dunestone breach

Custodian: [REDACTED]

Location: [REDACTED]

Status: Active, low profile recommended.

HE EXHALED, his whole body shaking.

She was alive.

Victoria was fucking *alive*.

Hidden, but someone—maybe even Victoria herself—had found a way to send him this breadcrumb. To tell him, *I'm still here.*

Jessie's voice shook him from his thoughts. "Spence?"

He snapped the laptop shut and turned to her. "Hey. Sorry. Didn't mean to wake you."

She blinked at him sleepily, but the edges of her mouth turned up. "Is it morning?"

"Close," he said. "Hospital coffee's terrible. Nurses confirmed it. How about more water?"

She gave a soft groan and adjusted her position. "You look like you've seen a ghost."

He hesitated, then said it aloud, reverent and shaken. "I found her."

"Found her...?" Jessie sat up suddenly as it sank in, grimacing through the pain. "Your sister?"

Everything in him was flush with adrenaline. "She was taken into protective custody. I don't know why, but they buried her so deep, she vanished. I got a message with a code, Vic609-bellcov. It's a clue. I traced it back to a failed MI5 shelter op tied to a black site relocation program. She's still under their protection."

Jessie's eyes filled with tears and something fiercer than hope. "You did it. Thank God."

Spence's throat closed. He wasn't the kind of man who cried. He'd locked that part of himself away too long ago to count.

But she reached out and wiggled her fingers, wanting his hand. He gave it to her, and she squeezed it tight. "You once told me I needed to believe in something bigger than revenge," she said softly. "Now it's your turn to believe in something bigger than failure."

He looked at her, at this woman who had once betrayed him and then rebuilt everything between them with grit and truth.

"I love you, J," he told her, because he needed to say it. Her lips parted, but he leaned forward, pressing his forehead gently to hers. "And I trust you with everything. Even her."

Her breath hitched. "I won't let you down again. I swear."

He chuckled. "I know that, and I'm ready for us to be partners in every sense of the word if you are." He motioned at the bed and the room. "Once you're back on your feet, that is."

She smiled through her tears, gently shoving him away and flipping the covers back. "Then let's go find your sister."

He stopped her, kissed her forehead, and grinned. "Not until the doctor okays it."

"But I'm ready now."

She wasn't even close, but he appreciated her tough, brave demeanor. He stroked her cheek. "Soon, luv." The only way to get her to rest was an obvious one. He lifted his arm in the sling. "When we're both in better shape."

She narrowed one eye at him. "Tomorrow, then?"

He laughed. "Tomorrow, I guess. Together."

She tugged him into the bed with her, holding him close and laying her head on his chest. Just outside the window, the sky began to lighten. "I'm happy."

The words came out sounding surprised. "Me, too," he said, and realized it was true.

For the first time in years, the silver coin in his pocket didn't feel like a goodbye.

It felt like a beginning.

He kissed the top of her head, reveling in the feel of her. "Me, too," he repeated.

Man Hunt

Man Killer

Man Down

Covert Affairs

Covert Tactics

Covert Obsession

Listen to the series on the Eleven Reader Publishing App!

The SCVC Taskforce Series

Deadly Pursuit

Deadly Deception

Deadly Force

Deadly Intent

Deadly Affair, A SCVC Taskforce novella

Deadly Attraction

Deadly Secrets

Deadly Holiday, A SCVC Taskforce novella

Deadly Target

Deadly Rescue

Deadly Bounty

Deadly Betrayal

Deadly Threat

The Super Agent Series

Operation Sheba

Operation Paris

Operation Proof of Life

Operation Lost Princess

Operation Ambush

Operation Contraband

Operation Sleeping With the Enemy

Operation Heist

The Justice Team Series with Adrienne Giordano

Stealing Justice

Cheating Justice

Holiday Justice

Exposing Justice

Undercover Justice

Protecting Justice

Missing Justice

Defending Justice

Schock Sisters Mystery Series w/Adrienne Giordano

1st Shock

2nd Strike

3rd Tango

4th Silence

The Secret Ingredient Culinary Mystery Series

The Secret Ingredient, A Culinary Romantic Mystery with Bonus Recipes

The Secret Life of Cranberry Sauce, A Secret Ingredient Holiday Novella

VISIT MY STORE

Did you know you can buy directly from me? When you do, the retailer doesn't take a cut and I can pass on the savings to YOU!

https://mistyevansbooks.com/shop

Benefits:

You can find ALL my books in one place

SAVE money

EARLY access to new releases

Special Collections, Boxed eSets, and Limited Editions

Support a small business (and support a dream!)

Why Buy Direct?

When you purchase a book by your favorite author, electronic or print, on retailer platforms, the company keeps 30-70% of the sale, leaving the author with little to no profit (after the company deducts delivery fees, taxes, and other fees).

Buying directly from the author means that more goes to them so they can keep turning out stories for you. Every published story, every book, requires cover art, editing, and hours and hours of the author's time simply to create it. Not to mention overhead costs, such as websites, newsletters, writing software, graphics programs, advertising, taxes, etc.

In addition, one of the big-name retailers requires exclusivity, and all of them have terms of service and rules and regulations that make it challenging and time-consuming for an indie author to navigate the publishing world.

Most of us would MUCH rather spend our time creating more stories for YOU, rather than trying to jump through the hoops at the retailers. Buying direct from your favorite authors (where available) helps ensure that an author you love is not subject to unexplained account closures, withholding of royalties, censorship, and other issues that can affect their livelihood.

I've experienced ALL of these. By buying direct, you help put control of my work back in my hands - and I can continue to write more.

Either way, thank you for supporting me! I under-stand buying direct doesn't work for everyone and even if you use the retailers to buy my books, I appreciate you!

Happy reading,

Misty

https://mistyevansbooks.com/shop

MEET MISTY

USA TODAY Bestselling Author Misty Evans is celebrating her 100th published novel in 2025. She loves writing urban fantasy, paranormal romance, and mystery/suspense. Under her pen name, Nyx Halliwell, she also writes supernatural cozy mysteries.

When not reading or writing (which is most of the time), she enjoys music, movies, and hanging out with her husband, twin sons, and three spoiled rescue dogs. She's a crafter at heart and has far too many projects to finish.

Visit www.mistyevansbooks.com to check out her online store and sign up for her newsletter.

NOTE FROM MISTY

Thank you for reading this story! It is an honor and a privilege to write books for you. I'm an indie author and every fan is important to me. I pour my heart into each story and do my best to bring you an escape from the real world.

Readers are the key to my success - not a traditional publishing deal (had four), an agent (had two), or a publicity team (yep, you guessed it, had several of those as well.)

Those of you who read my books, love my characters and worlds, and then tell others about them are the best of friends. I adore you and will keep writing if you keep reading!

If you'd like to learn about my other books, sales, and special promotions, please sign up for my newsletter at **www.mistyevansbooks.com**.

You'll get coupons to download starter packs for FREE, whether you love my suspense or my paranormal.

Support me directly (no retailer taking their cut), grab special edition box sets, and get new releases before they are out at retailers by visiting my store **https://mistye vansbooks.com/shop**.

I have sales and offer NEW RELEASES early! Check it out.

Last but not least, if you enjoy clean, cozy mysteries, visit my pen name **www.nyxhalliwell.com** to see those books.

Thank you, and happy reading!

Misty

I HAVE A SECRET TO SHARE
WITH YOU

Both of my grandmothers passed before I got to know them. I've spent my whole life longing for a grandmother's love and support.

From that longing, I've created Pearls of Wisdom from Gram, a weekly email with a small offering of encouragement and love from a grandmother figure. She's based on what I believe my grandmothers, Anna and Eunice, would say to me in this fast-paced, overwhelming world.

Are you an overwhelmed teacher, mother, or caregiver?

A nostalgic empty nester?

Or maybe a creative introvert?

I'm all of those things, and I've discovered that in this fast-paced world, sometimes all you need is the slow sipping of tea, a phrase that sticks with you all day, or a note that reminds you that your softness is a strength.

If your soul is craving rest, reflection, and tiny, meaningful rituals—*Pearls of Wisdom From Gram* might be just the thing.

Free subscribers get weekly "pearls of wisdom."

Paid subscribers get daily pearls right in their inbox. Wouldn't it be nice to get a word of encouragement every day?

You matter too much to run on empty.

♥ Subscribe now and take the first step toward a softer kind of support.

https://pearlsofwisdomfromgram.substack.com/

BECOME A FOUNDING SUPPORTER
OF MY FILMS BASED ON MY BOOKS!

I'm launching a new chapter in my creative career—*films based on my stories and brought to life* in TV-style series.

But I can't do this alone.

Each episode costs $200+ to produce. Turning a novel like Fatal Truth or Grim & Bare It into a full-length movie will cost upwards of $5,000.

My pilots for each series will most likely run $200-$500, as I have to learn as I go. It's an exciting time to dive in, and I'm studying film techniques so I can bring you *all the vibes.*

I want to see Trace and Savanna from Fatal Truth on screen.

And how about Chloe and Killion from my grim series?

Amy and Lucifer from Witches Anonymous? Yes, please!

If YOU want to see my sexy SEALs, kickass

urban fantasy heroines, or some juicy paranormal romance on your favorite screen (yes, you'll be able to watch them on your phone, computer, or TV), *I need your help to bring the pilot of my first shows to life.*

NOW is the time to join as a Founding Supporter of my pilot venture. Your name will be listed in the "Founding Supporters" section of the episode credits (or as "Anonymous" if preferred.)

Your contribution of $1, $20, or $100 goes *directly* into producing the episodes of my first series — and you'll receive special rewards and recognition for investing in my films.

If I meet my goals, EVERYONE WHO DONATES will get EARLY ACCESS to my pilot film(s), as well as receive several special bonuses from me, including the soundtracks (written and produced by me) that I use in the films.

You can learn more and pick a tier here: https://mistyevansbooks.com/become-a-founding-flame-help-launch-the-first-season-of-my-films   (You   MUST create an account or login to your preexisting one in order to donate.)

If you prefer not to set up an account, you can also donate directly by going here: https://buymeacoffee.com/MistyEvans/e/452907

OR donate via PayPal to beachpathpublishing@gmail.com

I'm so excited for this new adventure and I hope you'll be coming along on it with me!